Target: The White House!

The ex-Green Beret's face took shape on the oversize TV screen.

"Good morning, Mr. President. I expect you're waiting to find out what we meant when we said that something terrible *would* happen to Mrs. Charissa. Well...something terrible is *already* happening to her...."

Fighter planes scrambled from a Texas air force base soon confirmed the videotaped words. Mrs. Charissa, an airborne hostage bound and gagged, was visible through a window in the side of the huge plane. She was alone.

The pilotless craft was flying a suicide mission toward its computer-locked target...on Pennsylvania Avenue!

"Very, very action-oriented....Highly successful."
—*The New York Times*

Also available from Gold Eagle Books,
publishers of the Executioner series:

Mack Bolan's
ABLE TEAM

#1 Tower of Terror
#2 The Hostaged Island
#3 Texas Showdown
#4 Amazon Slaughter

Mack Bolan's
PHOENIX FORCE

#1 Argentine Deadline
#2 Guerilla Games
#3 Atlantic Scramble
#4 Tigers of Justice

MACK BOLAN

THE EXECUTIONER 51

BOLAN

Vulture's Vengeance

A GOLD EAGLE BOOK FROM

W⬤RLDWIDE

TORONTO · NEW YORK · LONDON

First edition March 1983

Special thanks and acknowledgment to
Patrick Neary for his contributions to this work.

ISBN 0-373-61051-3

Printed in Canada

"Never give in, never give in, *never, never, never, never*—in nothing great or small—never give in."
—*Sir Winston Churchill*

"We shall attack and attack until we are exhausted, and then we shall attack again."
—*Gen. George S. Patton Jr.*

"Yes, I am a soldier. I am the international soldier. The soldier of the land and the seas and the skies, for as long as evil shows its snakelike head, whenever and wherever. Peace is just an armistice in a war that lasts until the end of time."
—*Mack Bolan, The Executioner*
(from a letter to the President)

The Stony Man War-Room Team

of Mack Samuel Bolan, alias John Macklin Phoenix, retired Colonel, U.S.A., known as The Executioner a.k.a. Kicker, Striker, Stony Man One:

April Rose, primary mission controller and overseer of Stony Man's Virginia "Farm" HQ. Provides logistics, back-up support, loving care for the Phoenix people. Tall, lush-bodied, this shapely lady has been Mack Bolan's closest ally since The Executioner's final Days of De-Creation.

Hal Brognola, director of the Sensitive Operations Group, Stony Man liaison with the Oval Office. In his three-piece suit this ex-FBI agent looks like a vice-president of IBM. In fact he is a street-wise third-generation American who worked his own way into the stratosphere of the Justice Department's covert operations section. In that capacity he first met Mack Bolan. The rest is history.

Andrzej Konzaki, officially with Special Weapons Development, CIA, is unofficially attached to the Phoenix program. One of the most innovative armorers in the world. Master weaponsmith, expert on small arms, handguns to machine guns; knives; small explosives; other devices; and assigns them according to circumstances, locales. Legless since Vietnam. His CIA profile says: "Trust him."

Aaron "The Bear" Kurtzman, big, rumpled librarian of Stony Man's extensive electronic data bank, from which he interfaces with those of the National Security Council, the Justice Department, the CIA,

DIA and the intelligence agencies of every allied nation. Brilliant, a living extension of his computer. His tobacco-stained fingers dance over the console to call up mug shots, maps, raw data of all kinds.

Leo Turrin, Mob elder statesman (Leo "The Pussy" Turrin), undercover agent for Justice's Orgcrime Division, Washington lobbyist with connections, now officer of the Phoenix operation. From a *capo* on *La Commissione* to special friend and advisor to Bolan the blitz artist, this lieutenant of both the international underworld and sensitive operations walks a perilous path through the savage pastures.

Jack Grimaldi, combat pilot in Nam (137 missions, 2 Purple Hearts), later a flyboy for the Mob, now head of his own SOG cadre: G-Force. Can fly anything from a single-engine Scout to a Boeing 767, has proven himself to be Bolan's ace card on many missions. Of Italian parentage, is flamboyant, reckless, yet ruthlessly efficient. King of the sky.

Plus Tommy Anders, Toby Ranger, Smiley Dublin and others who are in constant touch with Stony Man's War Room, as are Mack Bolan's two tactical neutralization teams, Phoenix Force and Able Team.

The Phoenix program is a covert operation, unrecorded in the official records. Full U.S. government support makes the 160-acre Stony Man estate in the Shenandoah mountains the command center of the most formidable national security force ever assembled.

Dedicated to the tacticians of
the Air Force Antiterrorism Council,
whose determined work identifies
the "threat and vulnerability zones"
before death does.

PROLOGUE

From Mack Bolan's journal:

How FAR DO YOU GO to help a friend? The answer's got to be all the way. If you cannot go the last mile for him no matter what the cost, you cannot call yourself a friend.

Good men are getting fewer. When a person who has fought side by side with you against a common enemy is in trouble, you go the whole way for him, as hard as you can.

Each of us has the basic right not to be a victim, to live without fear. The price of civilization is the inhibition of good men's killer instincts. Most of us no longer know how to defend ourselves, let alone fight back.

The Animal men know this and use it against us, because they have no inhibitions whatsoever about smashing skulls or cutting throats or stabbing innocent people.

They're not squeamish, believe me. Why, then, should good men be so?

Maybe someday we'll have a civilization where no one will kill or maim. Until then, we're in a transition stage. I play a part in that transition. I fight to the death the vicious killers who prowl the jungle in packs. I do not do it for me, but for the weaker ones who are not able to fight for themselves.

It's time the killers realized that not one of their victims is so helpless as to be without a friend.

It's time they found out about The Executioner.

PHOENIX WAS MACK BOLAN'S NAME in this new war.

Phoenix—the bird that arose from its own ashes. In the sky was salvation from the miseries of the earth. And from the clouds, Phoenix could return like forked lightning. Translate that as: hard and deep penetration, deployable at zero notice.

Hit and git in hellrain. That was the idea, and it was not just theoretical. Mission after successful mission had proved that fact beyond any doubt. Mack the Fact.

"I have news for all those who think the world is going to hell," he wrote to the President of the United States. "They're dead wrong. The world already *has* gone to hell in large measure. The time for table talk has passed. At the end of the evening, the world is still in the same damn shape. It is time for action."

1

A CHILL TREMOR TICKLED the Executioner's spine.

Bolan left the engine running and waited. Seconds earlier he had parked the sleek silver sports car behind a late-model van on the tree-lined street. Late-afternoon sunlight filtered through the leaves of the trees behind him. Reflected light blazed off the mirror-treated rear windows of the van, the glare only slightly reduced by Bolan's sunglasses. He squinted to make out Delaware license plates and a legend painted on its back doors. "V.V.A.A." it proclaimed. Nothing else.

The van's engine suddenly rumbled to life. The vehicle lurched from the curb and was still accelerating as it screeched a right turn around the corner just past the next house. The driver ignored the stop sign there and was gone.

The Executioner's war knew no holidays anymore, yet to most of America on this particular day, a holiday was in progress. It was Saturday afternoon. Monday would be Memorial Day.

Mack Bolan had come to this small southern New Jersey town not to memorialize the dead, but to recall the living.

It might have seemed only a gesture to some: well-intentioned but essentially useless. He had come here to look in on a particular war veteran who had fallen on hard times.

Bolan killed the engine of the Corvette. He reached behind the passenger seat for the six-pack perspiring in the shadows there.

The beer was for a buddy. A buddy, to Bolan, was anyone who fought the good fight.

Bobby Latchford fit that bill. He had until just lately, anyway. Latchford had distinguished himself in Vietnam, back during Bolan's days of military service there. His DEROS from Nam heralded the start of a strong career. He soon made sergeant in Philadelphia's tough police force, not an easy task. His relatively smooth move back into stateside life had made him a model of veteran readjustment. Through the VA he gave freely of his time and energy to share that transformation with less fortunate vets, who had gotten stuck in the threshold between hell and health.

But something happened, or maybe nothing happened, and Bobby, too, fell to hell.

A lot of people wondered why. So did Mack Bolan.

The question had brought him here to this run-down neighborhood, to this run-down little house and, he feared, to a run-down man.

Bolan's fingers strayed from the beer to linger on another object, its handle chilled from its riding position next to the six-pack.

This day, especially, it was Mack Bolan's silent, solemn wish that the Beretta stay that way: cool.

He picked up his shoulder holster, quickly removed his blue denim shirt, slipped the holster on and slid the chilled new Beretta 93-R snug into leather. He put his shirt back on and left the buttons undone. Six-pack in hand, he stepped out of the car.

In a moment he would be standing on the front porch of a guy who was bound not to know him after all these years. Bolan's new face would hardly jog the memory of a man who had not seen him since before the Mafia war.

In truth it was Bolan who hardly knew Latchford, even in the Vietnam days. They were acquainted with each other more by reputation than by actual time spent together. In person they had met once, briefly. In fact, for all he knew, Bobby Latchford might have been one of the cops who had nearly blown him off a telephone pole back in that alley in Philadelphia. One night he'd pushed the numbers too far and found himself in the police spotlight, literally.

Latchford's name had shown up recently in a computer listing of possible recruits for the Stony Man forces. He had survived the multiple cross-sorting that had reduced the list to fewer than sixty men with the highest qualifications. Each of these men had done heroic service in Vietnam and had pursued varied lives after it. Their success or failure in the civilian world did not necessarily have a bearing on Stony Man's judgment of them—just its curiosity about them. A man could fall from grace and still be most useful to the Executioner's kind of war.

Bolan climbed the sagging porch steps and approached the door.

A note, scrawled and faded, was taped above the doorbell button. "Broke," it read. "Knock hard."

Muted shuffling sounds emanated from within the bungalow. At Bolan's knock they ceased.

New sounds floated around from the rear of the place. A screen door slammed, an engine started. Finally, a pair of voices quarreled in strained whispers. The argument was brief. He recognized the language as some Hispanic variation.

Bolan decided a look-see was in order.

Stepping off the porch, he made his way through the unfenced side yard, climbed quietly around the clutter of parched lumber and rusting automobile parts, rotting legacies of some more ambitious day.

He set the six-pack down on an old engine block. From the sound of things, he didn't expect to find a picnic going on back there.

Neither did he expect to see another van, identical to the first one. Somewhere within its mirrored glass an anxious driver gunned the throttle repeatedly.

Four-inch-high block lettering on the side panel explained what V.V.A.A. stood for: Vietnam Veterans for Affirmative Action.

A dark young man in baggy khakis was running toward the van, awkwardly trying to balance a half-filled duffel bag on one shoulder and a pair of M-16s on the other.

Bolan read and re-read the situation, but none of the readings would play.

He unholstered the Beretta.

He held the weapon behind his back, out of sight but ready.

"Hey, Bobby! That you?" he called out, knowing it wasn't.

A slight creaking from the screen door on his left sent Bolan's eyes flashing. A split second later he executed a fast dive into the dense dead grass. In that same rolling motion he brought the 93-R to arm's length aim. By this time the guy at the door had pulled the trigger on a .45 automatic. Hot lead split the air where the Executioner had been standing only an instant before.

The Beretta replied with a quiet *phut-phut*. A couple of 9mm mosquitoes bored through the screen door. The bites were fatal. A lifeless body pushed the door wide open and tumbled down the steps into its final sprawl.

The Beretta tracked back to the first man, who had dropped the duffel bag and was foolishly aiming an M-16 in Bolan's direction.

The Beretta spit shamelessly and the khaki man flew backward. His ears were never witness to death's quiet knock.

The van had already jerked into motion by the time the little man's dead body banged against it, the rear wheels biting for purchase in the gravel of the alleyway.

Aiming at an invisible driver through silvered windows required as much a gut instinct as an educated guess. Under tutored guidance the Beretta sneezed twice more in quiet righteousness. The van reacted to the uninvited 9mm hitchhikers by mowing down a sagging picket fence and ricocheting off a utility pole, before it plowed into a small toolshed on the opposite side of the gravel lane.

The collision ignited spare gasoline in the ramshackle shed. Instantly flames spread into the van.

Bolan was there a moment later, peering through shattered windows at the driver, visible now. The guy looked at Bolan with a mixture of fear and hatred, but mostly fear. His right ear was missing, as was a chunk of his scalp, bleeding testaments to Bolan's marksmanship.

The driver's eyes were shifting wildly back and forth from Bolan to his own legs, pinned under the dashboard and already singed by the approaching flames.

"Where is Bobby Latchford?" demanded Ice Eyes.

But it was useless.

The guy angrily shouted something in Spanish.

"Make sense or I make you dead," commanded the cool man.

The fool guy's eyes suddenly shifted to a pistol on the passenger-side floor. He lunged for it.

The Executioner made him dead.

Mack Bolan turned and strode back to the little house. It was only ninety seconds earlier that he had knocked on Bobby Latchford's front door.

He stepped over a still-bleeding body and through the back door of the bungalow.

So this is how a once-brave soldier lived, he thought, saddened.

It did not take long to check out the whole place. It was obvious that Bobby was not there, though there was evidence he had been.

Bolan unlatched the front door and went out.

An American flag, sun-faded, flew from a standard affixed to the porch pillar. It was, Bolan noted, the only flag on the block.

He walked to the 'Vette. Sirens approached now, and he put the silver sports car in motion and left the place behind him.

He was committed now, drawn into the life of a guy he hardly knew.

This was going to be one hell of a Memorial Day weekend.

2

ROUGHLY MIDWAY between New York City and Washington, D.C., at the bottom end of the New Jersey turnpike, there is a bridge connecting southeastern New Jersey to the state of Delaware and all other points west. Actually there are two bridges. They are identical and stand within a few hundred feet of each other. The twin spans share a single name: Delaware Memorial Bridge.

Approaching the bridge from the north, Bolan's Corvette took less than a minute to pass through the entire length of the little town of Deepwater. The town marks the point at which the Delaware River deepens and widens out, eventually becoming the Delaware bay that opens into the Atlantic Ocean. Although small as towns go, Deepwater is home to one of the largest chemical plants in the world.

Shortly after passing the plant's main entrance, Bolan moved onto the bridge approach and weaved his way through the holiday traffic.

Each of the twin bridges was one-way. The flow of cars and trucks moved freely enough for him to squeeze through the gaps at speed. When he had nearly reached the crest, however, the traffic stopped abruptly, then briefly started again. Finally nothing moved, the Corvette included.

Those last few car-lengths had made some difference. Now it was possible to see down the far side of the bridge.

Bolan's powerful binoculars, which had been stashed beneath the seat, soon showed him exactly what he had hoped to see—a dusty silver-windowed van. It was stopped just short of a rear-end collision farther down the bridge. The crash had effectively blocked all four lanes, with the exception of a narrow space at the right end of the bridge apron.

The van was attempting to bluff its way toward that space, starting and stopping impatiently. A man leaned out the passenger-side window, shouting and making threatening gestures intended to convince other drivers to clear the way. The man's anger seemed to build as he was routinely ignored.

Bolan dropped the binoculars onto the seat beside him, grabbed up the massive AutoMag and its holster belt from behind the seat and clinched it around his waist. Then he leaped out of his car, bent on breaking whatever records might exist for fastest downhill run on a bridge, Memorial or otherwise.

Behind him and fading fast were the angry shouts and blasting horns of motorists who would never understand why some jackass had just abandoned a brand-new sports car in the middle of their vacation path.

The van advanced a space closer to the hole through the jam.

Then the passenger was out of the van, standing by a yellow station wagon that had refused to yield, pounding on its hood. The wagon's driver became cavalierly righteous and got out of his car. Without further ado the van passenger smashed a hard right fist into the motorist's face.

Again the van moved ahead and its belligerent passenger started back to rejoin it. As he pulled open the door, the guy glanced back to find the injured man following him, a tire iron in hand. Despite the shouted pleas of his wife and shrill screams of terror from his children, the motorist continued to press for a confrontation.

The look on his face turned sour as he doubled over with a hot bullet tearing through his gut. He dropped to his knees, swayed for a moment, then toppled to the pavement.

Bolan reached the station wagon at the same moment, AutoMag drawn.

The Executioner drew an instant bead on the guy scrambling back into the van. A quick scan of the situation, and he thought better of it. Too many people, too much spilled gasoline from the wreck, and maybe—probably—Bobby Latchford in the van, willingly or otherwise.

The van lurched again, this time making it through the gap by tearing the rear fender off one of the crashed cars and roaring away toward the toll plaza.

The AutoMag slipped back into place on Bolan's hip as he dashed ahead to the gap.

The next car in line was a red MG convertible with the top down and a young bikinied blonde behind the wheel. When he placed his hand on the top edge of her door, the eyes that met Bolan's were almost as blue but considerably less icy. Still, they were cool. Pretty lips parted slightly in surprise.

Wordlessly she pulled the parking brake and moved herself over the brake-and-shift console and into the passenger seat, where she stubbornly remained.

Bolan jumped in without opening the door. There was no time to fight her stubbornness. He dropped the brake lever, then burned her car through the gap.

He swerved to avoid the first arriving bridge patrol cruiser, missing its tail end by a tight inch.

Ahead, alarm bells began ringing as the dusty van barged its way through one of the toll booths.

The Executioner was not planning to stop either. He swung the small British roadster toward the outside lane and roared through the orange highway pylons that blocked the lane to law-abiding motorists. One of the plastic pylons stuck beneath the car for a moment, until friction melted its resistance and it tumbled away.

Bolan kept his eyes on the speeding van until it disappeared around the bend of an exit ramp. The sign read Airport.

The few seconds it took for the little MG to reach the ramp gave Bolan time to take a first good look at his passenger.

She was not as young as the teenager he had first taken her for. Mid-twenties probably. He couldn't help noticing her legs, but he did not linger there nor anywhere else along the curving route to her still-chilled eyes.

The girl found her voice. It was right behind the lump in her throat. "Y-you a cop?"

"No."

"Oohhh."

She slumped back a little deeper in the seat and folded nicely tanned arms across her chest.

Bolan downshifted and hurled the little car into the curve of the exit ramp. The MG hurtled out of the bend with the engine whining and the needle of the tachometer well over the red line. He quick-shifted into fourth.

"It's new, you know," she said on the car's behalf. She made a point of not looking at him.

"I guess you wish you were somewhere else right now," Bolan grunted.

"It crossed my mind," came the cool reply.

He noticed a half-thumbed paperback book resting on the dashboard against the windshield, a romance. *Hot Holiday* proclaimed its cover. Beneath the title was an illustration of lovers on a secluded beach.

"Read a lot?" he asked, indicating the book with a slight nod.

"Listen mister, I don't *believe* you. There's been a shooting on the bridge, you steal my car, abduct me, the cops are behind us and God knows what kind of murdering criminals are ahead of us in that van. And you got a gun like I've never seen strapped to your belt and you're not a cop, and all you can say is do I like to read? Who the hell are you, anyway?"

She was fuming, but still she avoided his gaze.

"There wasn't time to explain. You're right about those guys in the van. They are murderers—"

"You don't need to tell me that. You're not a cop—then what, a Fed?"

"I'm an army colonel. Retired."

She looked at him with wide eyes. His statements of fact only made him more mysterious. And this high-speed chase was veering toward the terminally dangerous.

The car screamed after the van along a road that curved into the outer perimeter of the airport. Bolan was almost on the tail of the van when it swerved around the corner of a hangar.

Bolan took the corner in a sliding right-hand power turn that seriously challenged the little MG's ability to hold fast to *terra firma*. The smell of fresh burned rubber rushed into his nostrils. A split-second later it was mixed with another fragrance, that of perfumed blond hair, as the girl lost her grip on the dashboard and was pressed screaming against his right shoulder.

As she slammed into him, her left knee kicked out reflexively, knocking the gear lever into neutral and cutting off power to the rear wheels. The tiny sports car instantly developed an understeer, sending it wide of a narrow gate and directly toward a chain link fence.

Bolan pushed the girl back into her seat and laid himself across her as the MG tore through the fence. The bottom of the fence gave way first, raking its lower edge across the top of the car, a fence post half-flattening out the windshield support and shattering the safety glass into a shower of pea-size pellets that rained onto their huddled bodies.

The car kept moving. The Executioner snapped back behind the wheel and rammed the stick into second gear. Whirling the wheel to right lock, he stamped the accelerator pedal down to squeal around a parked Cessna, then ripped rubber right on back to the road surface.

The van was still in sight. It had skidded hastily to a brief stop, narrowly avoiding a collision with an overnight-express courier van that had unwittingly cruised into the battle path. Now the dusty V.V.A.A. truck noisily cranked through the gears to get back up to speed.

The killer leaned out the passenger side window. There was no mistaking the angry look on the creep's face, even at this distance. The guy proceeded to haul out an AK-47 and aim to the rear. At Bolan.

The big guy in the little car was already a step ahead of him, unsheathing the AutoMag and pointing it through what had been a windshield.

The girl started to sit up.

"Get down," he commanded icily, without looking at her.

She obediently huddled herself into a fetal ball against the dashboard and stifled a scream as the giant AutoMag exploded percussively to dispatch *mucho* grains of dead-end lead.

The head exploded and disappeared from the van's window. Bolan swerved slightly to avoid running over the abandoned AK-47 as it came to rest on the roadway.

The girl was hysterical now, tears streaming down her face.

Bolan wanted to comfort her. A large part of him wanted to tell her everything was all right.

But everything was not all right. At the moment, he had an MG in his left hand and the hawgleg of death in his right. It had to be first things first, and even the smallest time-out was an invitation to suicide.

The back doors of the van suddenly cracked open slightly and a flaming red firespike leaped from the darkness inside.

Mack Bolan recognized the sound that accompanied that light. It was a grenade launcher and at this range it was too late to avoid its deadly issue.

The grenade tracked low and struck the left front tire. It detonated immediately and with such force that the lightweight sports car was kicked over onto its right-side two wheels. It balanced there precariously at forty miles an hour for the largest part of a second, before finally crashing back onto its wheels to a halt.

Bolan swiftly leaped over the undamaged door on his side onto the pavement.

The van was gone. He holstered the big AutoMag. Leaning back into the damaged car for the girl, he clasped her hand in his, but she was hurt, hurt real bad, and she did not respond.

He lifted her supple body in his arms and walked to the side of the roadway and gingerly laid her on the pavement. He covered her semi-naked upper body with his shirt.

"You're gonna be okay," he said to her closed eyes. He felt the rage rise in him, the fury at innocence defiled, the universal anger against the blood that flows from the bystander, and from the young, and from the sinless.

Already men were running toward the extraordinary crash scene. Bolan knew there were enough questions to be asked about all this that he could afford to risk disappearing in the crush.

Feeling for her pulse to establish that the girl's recovery was assured, Bolan bid her farewell. "I have always tried to keep innocent people out of my war," he whispered to her gently breathing form. "War is the feast of vultures, and you're no meal for death. Take care."

With that, he leaped up and ran for the nearest hangar, long-legging it past the arriving strangers.

"I have to call," he shouted at them, as if to indicate that he would call the police.

But he would make no such call. This scene of catastrophe would have to be dealt with by the onlookers; there were ambulances and police within whistling distance.

It was the Executioner's ambition now to melt into the fabric of the airport and only reappear when he was safely on course to the War Room, where this matter must be resolved.

His skills at the arts of war ensured the success of his escape, away from a suddenly war-shattered site in a part of town that no doubt thought it was at peace.

For its own sake, it should think again.

War was everywhere now.

3

A VOICE SAID, "Here we are, sir.... Sir?"

Bolan opened his eyes and nodded grimly to the young National Guard pilot. He reached out to release the latch but the door was already swinging open. Looking up, he met Jack Grimaldi's smiling eyes. Bolan flashed a grin briefly, but the somberness returned as he climbed out of the helicopter.

"Hey-hey, howya been, buddy?" Grimaldi, somehow, could be cheerful in almost any situation, even during a call to war. Jack slammed the door shut and motioned for the copter to be gone.

The two started across to Stony Man Farm's big house.

In the War Room, April rushed over to Mack Bolan for a greeting. Business dictated that it be brief. She sighed almost inaudibly as they broke away.

Bolan's presence dominated the room as soon as he had entered. With some weariness he seated himself at the table. It was only now that the meeting could properly begin.

Hal Brognola, the White House liasion, lightly held the telephone to his ear. Except for his occasional grunts, the only other sound in the War Room was the muffled activity of a busy computer printer.

The others were already gathered around the table. None looked happy, a condition that had absolutely nothing to do with having a holiday weekend cut short. Not this group. These were professionals, every one, to the core, and they were fighting a war. War carves its own calendar.

Leo Turrin quietly pulled out a fresh cigar and trimmed it. He produced a slim gold lighter from his pocket, lit up, and leaned back in his chair, pensive. Turrin was an officer of the Phoenix program, but outside this room and beyond the electrified fences and defenses of Stony Man Farm, he operated under one level or other of his cover. In the underworld he was a "semi-retired" mob chieftain, and to the rest of the world he was a well-connected Washington lobbyist.

"Havana?" asked Aaron "The Bear" Kurtzman.

"You mean the cigar or the situation?" replied Turrin, with the hint of a smile. "As for the cigar, of course not. The situation—I don't know."

Hal replaced the receiver.

"High stakes," Brognola began. "Details are still sketchy at the moment. A commando raid in Panama, about six o'clock our time. The terrorists tried to kidnap John Leonard Charissa, our ambassador to the United Nations. He and his wife were down there on a goodwill tour. He was shot. Accidentally, we think. They left him and took his wife instead."

"Anna Charissa!" The news evidently disturbed April. It was true that Anna Charissa was probably better known to the general public than her diplomat husband. Her beauty, candor and outspokenness on the subject of human rights had gained her a popularity that transcended national borders.

April had met Anna several years earlier, and the impression was as lasting on her as it was on the many millions of others who shared Anna Charissa's dream. April was an NSA guest at a San Diego conference on torture and political imprisonment, and had been very taken with her co-delegate's beauty and evident inner strength. Anna was a lady with a job to do, and a big one—to make the world fit for human habitation. But April Rose had been annoyed immediately by the way so many men and even women responded only to Anna's admittedly remarkable body. To Anna, and to April, the body is merely the vehicle in which the soul moves about on this planet, and it was Anna's soul that had something to say, not her body. Those who misunderstood this failed to understand what her life was about. Anna Charissa's life was about Truth, not Beauty.

"Do we know who the kidnappers are?" asked Leo Turrin.

Brognola replied with a frustrated shrug. "At least four or five helicopters were used for their escape—"

"Good," said Kurtzman. "That narrows down our list of suspects, doesn't it?"

"Theoretically, yes," said Brognola.

"But?" put in Bolan.

"But early reports claim the choppers were dressed in U.S. markings. Probably phony paint, but right now we don't know with any certainty."

"Is the military missing any aircraft?" asked Jack Grimaldi.

"None that they know of, but all branches are running a thorough double-check," replied Hal. "I should say no helicopters are missing. Air force reports a Herky-Bird C-130 prop transport seems to have disappeared from Howard AFB in the Canal Zone, but that was over a month ago and may not be related."

He paused, pulled on his cigar.

"There is another twist, and frankly I'm not sure what to make of it. Apparently these commandos were wearing Green Beret uniforms, which is probably how they were able to get so close to—"

Grimaldi interrupted angrily. "Hal, you're wasting your time if you think those assholes are American soldiers."

No one disagreed.

The telephone buzzed at Hal's elbow.

"Brognola," he said brusquely. He listened for seconds, then hung up without a word, swiveled his chair to the console behind him and punched some buttons.

On the opposite wall of the War Room a large video screen arose from floor level. Simultaneously the room's lights dimmed. Beside the console a video-cassette machine clicked into operation, preparing to record an incoming transmission.

"That was the Agency," Hal explained. "A ransom demand has been received. It seems our terrorists are very up-to-date. The demand was transmitted electronically. On video."

"Tape or broadcast?" asked Kurtzman. "And from where?"

"Videotape cassette, anonymously delivered to a television station in Mexico City, I'm told. Delivered from *where* is anybody's guess. The Mexicans beamed it by satellite to Washington on one of the Pentagon's special channels, only minutes ago. The Agency is feeding it here now."

The picture began taking shape, in black and white, on the video projection screen. The quality was poor, even by amateur standards, but the message was alarmingly clear.

A Green Beret "sergeant" appeared, in uniform,

and identified himself by name and serial number. In a dull, emotionless voice he demanded one hundred million dollars "on behalf of the thousands of mistreated Vietnam veterans, both here and in the United States."

The American government, he said, was to deposit the money into a numbered Swiss account by noon of the next day, Washington time. Unless the demands were met, "something terrible" would happen to Anna Charissa. What that something was would be revealed before the deadline.

The screen went blank.

The phone buzzed again.

"Yeah?" Brognola grunted twice and hung up.

"Okay, the computers have verified the guy's ID. He's for real. Sergeant Larry Shortner, just like he said. Marines, honorable discharge. He disappeared about six weeks ago. And so did several other vets he was known to associate with."

"I sure don't like the implications," said Leo Turrin.

"Yeah, well neither do I," raged Grimaldi. "And I'll tell you something. I know lots of guys who fought in that war. So does Sarge. Sure, most of them don't like the way they've been treated since they got back. It sucks, we all know that. But guys with brains enough to pull off a stunt like this wouldn't be stupid enough to do it in the first place. Am I right?"

"Cool down, Jack," said Leo.

"Am I right?" he repeated.

"Jack's got a damn good point," Bolan interjected calmly, without elaboration.

The room fell quiet for a long moment, then Kurtzman spoke up.

"I agree," he said, "on the basis of the evidence we just witnessed. An action like this would surely destroy any chance for sympathy from the American public, and even a hundred million dollars won't make up for that. Things will get worse for vets, not better. And there's something else that bothers me. The Swiss banks aren't open on Sundays, are they? I think we could be dealing with a really marginal fringe element here, a small group sufficiently frustrated and angry enough to—"

"That's right, and I'm telling you," Grimaldi insisted hotly, "there's an insurrectionist mind behind this, not some poor soldiers with good intentions."

"Even so," Leo Turrin said evenly, "that doesn't rule out Americans as mercenaries."

Bolan stood up. "Let's agree to disagree until some real facts turn up, my friends. Whoever or whatever they are, we don't have much time. We start in Panama. I'll need a jet—"

"No problem, pal," offered Grimaldi.

Bolan held a palm up at Grimaldi's interruption. "—and an air force pilot," he concluded.

Jack was speechless, crushed.

Bolan looked the guy square in the eye.

Grimaldi tried to pull himself together, but it hurt. "Okay, okay. So I get a little hot sometimes, so what? I ain't made for talkin' good. I'm made for flyin' and fightin'."

Grimaldi was out of the chair now, pacing and doing his best to hide the moisture forming in his eyes. He was an emotional guy, sure. But actual outbursts like this were rare, and he wasn't sure how to handle the damn thing.

"But," he continued, trying to force some stability back into his voice, "if you guys think I'm gonna sit around with my trigger finger up my nose when there's a job to do, then...then...."

He didn't know what else to say, except *I've blown it*.

"I guess I blew it," he said.

"Nope," said Bolan, getting up and going over to him. "You're good, Jack. The best. I need you to find Bobby Latchford for me," he said.

The other four men and one woman in the darkened room all reacted to the name in silence. They were still in a degree of shock from Hal's report on Mack's bloody run-in with hell that morning.

"Aw, hell, Sarge," said Grimaldi. "Some drunk you hardly know? Can't the cops handle it?"

Bolan resisted icing up, but Jack was making it hard. "Jack, Bobby Latchford is important."

Bolan did not take his eyes off Grimaldi's.

Grimaldi surrendered.

"I've been a jerk, definitely non-pro. I'm sorry, Mack. Of course I'll do it."

Bolan placed both hands on the flier's firm shoulders. "No apologies needed here. Thanks, buddy."

"I'll get right on it, Sarge." Jack Grimaldi smiled warmly, nodded to the others and left the room.

"Okay, let's get me to Panama pronto." Bolan turned to the others. "Hal, there are some things you could check out for me. Find out what kind of choppers they used and their fuel-range radius. And see what you can find out about this V.V.A.A. organization...I've never heard of them."

"Neither have I," added the Fed.

"When you find out, be sure to let Jack know as well."

War carved its own calendar. Memorial Day

weekend had been shot to hell by a bunch of potential assassins, and the schedule was now number ten.

With an AO spreading wide like a pool of blood.

4

"WE HAVE COMPANY, Colonel Phoenix. Four o'clock low."

Bolan looked over his right shoulder into the black air.

"Read our location, Major."

"Latitude 82.4 west, longitude 14.91 north. Heading one-niner-one at 720 knots air, 660 ground. ETA 0200 hours, approximate."

"How high are we?"

"Altitude, fifteen thousand, sir. We began a slow descent several minutes ago."

"What's below us, Major?"

"I make us about fourteen minutes past the Honduras-Nicaragua border, sir. Niner miles off blue feature, south of Puerto Cabezas."

"Then you make our visitors Nicaraguan?"

"Most likely, sir. Radar counts three visitors."

"Are we in international airspace?"

"Affirmative...technically speaking. Excuse me, Colonel. They're coming up, sir."

"Hang tight, Major. Maintain course and speed."

In less than a moment, two jets came abreast, one to either side.

The pilot's voice crackled through the intercom again. "I make no markings, sir."

Indeed, the jets were painted flat black, almost

indistinguishable from the darkness itself. Night fighters. But whose?

"Super Sabres," Bolan told the pilot. "F-100s. Very old, almost ancient. Some countries still use them. So did we in Nam."

The black jet on the right drifted closer, less than thirty yards from their F-4's wing tips.

"You think he's trying to tell us something, Colonel?"

A flash of fire flared from the nose of the Super Sabre on the left, tracer bullets that punctuated the night like neon.

"I don't like the message," said Bolan.

The mystery pilot then repeatedly flashed a small light from his cockpit.

"Colonel Phoenix, that's international Morse code and he's spelling d-o-w-n. And there's more—he says a third jet is directly on our six aiming a heat-seeker. I must call in, sir."

The pilot switched frequencies and made his report, then came back on.

"Help is on the way from the carrier *Nimitz*, but that's fifty miles northeast of our position. ETA eight minutes. This bird can lose those old fighters almost instantly, sir, but procedure says we sit tight for the moment."

"You're the pilot in command, Major."

APRIL ROSE picked up the phone.

"Texas! Jack, I thought you were in New Jersey or Delaware."

"I work fast," came the flier's reply. "And from the looks of things I won't be here in the Lone Star much longer either."

"What have you come up with, Jack?"

"When I got to the airport back in Delaware, I started talking to some of the ground crew. I found this one guy, he's a vet himself. Turns out he did see that van tonight, near the crash-and-kill site. He said he'd seen a similar vehicle before and at that time walked over to see what the Vietnam Veterans for Affirmative Action was all about. He told them it sounded like an organization he'd like to join up with. He got a pretty rude reception. They told him to beat it, that the organization was all full up."

"Any identification?" asked April. "Was the guy he talked to an American?"

"Yeah, an American red-blooded type, but pretty high-strung, nervous. Said something about membership was by invitation only and also mentioned something about having to meet the 'Yareem standard.' "

"You mean the marine standard."

"No, the ground-crew guy asked the same question. They didn't spell it out to him, but they did tell him to shove off fast. There's big money involved here, looks like," added Grimaldi. "The Delaware guy saw the same bunch of guys get into a Lear jet and take off. Said he overheard the plane's pilot mention Texas, but the rest was in Spanish."

"Mercenaries?"

"I hate to admit it, but it stacks up that way. The Sarge isn't going to like the idea of his friend Latchford being hooked up in this. I'd have to say the kidnapping angle is dead. Here's another choice bit of news. The Lear had a South American registry number, Colombia I think, unless it was phonied up. Here's the number. You check it for me."

April made a note of the number, said: "And you tailed the plane to Texas?"

"Yeah, but I lost it on the ground. This is a big

field here. My best guess is that they gassed up and split again already. There's a lotta Lears leaving here all the time, a lot more than in Delaware.''

"What next, Jack?''

"Just figure I'm on my way to Colombia. That plane had oversized tip tanks. Run the registration number for me as soon as you can. Anything comes up, you got my frequency.''

Hanging up the phone, April wondered what kind of impact the news about Bobby would have on Mack Bolan.

One remarkable thing about Mack, she knew, was his capacity to take bad news and somehow make it work for him, to make it sharpen his edge. How did he do it?

He was about to have to do it again.

She caught Brognola's eyes and indicated she had a message for Stony Man One.

The Fed nodded. His face looked more grim than usual, she noticed.

He went on with his phone conversation. "I don't like the looks of it, either. You should have had an escort to begin with, but that's neither here nor there now.... I know, I know, and I agree with you, of course. The international political aspects—well, you're just as valuable to us in that regard. Use your best judgment, Striker. If you have to use force—any degree of force—to keep yourself in working order, you'll be backed up totally. You know that. Hang on a second for April.''

"Hal, stay on the line,'' April said, picking up her phone again and punching in the lighted button. "You'll want to hear this too. Mack, what's happening—are you—''

"Hal will fill you in later," came Bolan's reply. "Got news to report?"

"Yes, from Jack. It's about Bobby. He says it's not definitive, but you ought to know that the V.V.A.A. is more than likely a front for mercenaries. Jack said your kidnapping theory is not looking good in Latchford's case. But he'll stay on the trail unless you say otherwise."

Bolan took the news silently.

"I guess if something comes up, Jack can use his discretion?" she said finally. "Mack, does the 'Yareem standard' mean anything to you?"

Bolan's end of the line went dead.

5

NORMALLY, an F-4 is a formidable aircraft. One version claimed a time-to-climb speed of 19,000 feet in fifty seconds. From a standing start on the runway.

This was a Lockheed built for twice the speed of sound.

The craft's official nickname is Phantom, but the men who fly it have come up with a couple of others. The favorite seems to be "The Flying Brick." As in, "Put a big enough engine on it and even a brick will fly."

To fully protect the F-4's extensive—and expensive—equipment would require quite a bit of armor, and more armor equals less payload and reduced agility. The design decision to lighten the armor plate no doubt took into consideration the plane's remarkable flying characteristics. Raw speed and its ability to outfly most pursuers are persuasive qualities, and there is the argument that armor plate is of little defense against today's weapons, most notably heat-seeking air-to-air missiles.

A fully loaded weapons configuration including a 20mm gun, Sidewinder and Sparrow missiles, as well as bombs, brings the "Brick's" average takeoff weight up to a maximum total of 16,000 pounds.

The decision to use these weapons remains with the pilot in command. He is beset at all times with a range shortened by high fuel consumption. In so-called "peacetime," such decisions can be difficult. At some level of consciousness at least, every military pilot with his finger poised on a trigger knows that his might be the finger that pushed the button that starts the beginning of the end.

It is, therefore, heady stuff.

There are guidelines, of course. But in the final analysis, individual pilot responsibility cannot be avoided.

Whatever the reputation of modern military pilots as "hotshots" or "joystick jockeys," the reality behind the image is more sober. Those hell-raiser reputations, more often than not, were earned on the ground.

Coming down after flight, these men return to earth with a perspective few ground-bound souls can imagine. For one, they love their jobs. For another, there is an exuberance that cannot easily be contained, born as it is of the sheer exhilaration of flying like an eagle. It is no wonder they sometimes act superior—they probably feel like butterflies among all the caterpillars.

And not least, there is a release, once back on the ground, from the demanding discipline that is required at every moment that their craft is in the skies. A flier has little liberty to allow his mind to wander, but the temptation, the seduction, is always there, waiting to consume him. At the speeds and altitudes involved, a mistake in procedure or judgment—a mere molehill of error—can in seconds turn into a mountain; literally, with a multimillion-dollar airplane smeared for miles across its craggy bulk.

Like it or not, fliers are married to that bitch, gravity. The sky is actually only a mistress, very exciting but by necessity limited to brief interludes.

Like a lover, the air cannot be possessed, only temporarily experienced.

Passengers or copilots, under normal conditions, were under considerably less pressure.

Under normal conditions, sure.

THE SLEEK JET BUCKED. An accompanying dull hammering announced the arrival of lethal lead issue as several of the marauders' multimillimeter calling-cards came ripping through the forward port side of the cockpit.

The main radio, the hook with the ground, was immediately eliminated by the first rounds.

The air force pilot had responded to the invasion by pushing the fast mover into a steep, rolling power dive. Curiously, he did not seem inclined to pull out of it.

"Major?" said Bolan. Then he realized the guy was not particularly talkative either. He was dead.

The inside of the forward canopy was a mess of red from the direct hit that had traveled through the lower edge of the canopy and into the pilot's left ear.

Bolan would never get used to death arriving within arm's reach, however often in the hellgrounds it occurred.

Now he fought the stick back with some effort, managing at last to pry the controls from the death grip of the dead pilot up front.

The plane plunged on into its barrel-rolling death dive. Time was tugging on eternity's trigger as somewhere in the darkness below, a whole ocean rushed up.

The flat black pursuers had continued to follow, diving deeply to match the crippled craft, smelling the odor of imminent death and eager to confirm or even induce its arrival.

The Executioner was fully on the stick now, goosing the small left aileron to counteract the roll, thereafter straining the stick back and to starboard. His feet found the pedals and pushed for hard right rudder.

The falling brick became a plane again, obedient to its new master, veering off to the right at a dangerously low altitude, heading due west.

The dark fighters followed tight on the rear like mad dogs on a mailman.

Bolan's position in the back seat of the Phantom prevented him from seeing much in front of it. A few scattered lights were now passing below on what he judged to be the eastern coastline of Nicaragua.

He reckoned his current position as somewhere south of the Mosquito coast, maybe two or three dozen miles below the port city of Puerto Cabezas. There would be marshland in this area, and few inhabitants. And farther on, if he remembered his geography, would come forest, jungle and the rocky badlands.

The few instruments still in working condition were not telling him anything he wanted to know. Pressure was low and kept falling. The throttle was inoperable, a casualty of the original hit. There was no way to speed up and only a few ways of slowing down, all of them drastic.

Ordinarily the plane was highly maneuverable. But without real power behind it, the plane lacked the agility needed to shake off the hounds.

More glowing tracers streaked past. Bolan took some comfort in the relative immaturity of his pursuers as aerial marksmen.

The Phantom continued slowing down on its stabilized path, and the controls were becoming increasingly limp. Several of the backup systems either failed or had been hit. The thing was fast devolving back into a brick.

Mack Bolan's flying experience, of considerably less duration than his car-driving miles, had taught him one thing he would never forget: that the most important difference between an airplane and an automobile is the space between the ground and one's hindquarters. If ever that space gets to be not so different anymore, it's time to quit flying.

"This just ain't my style, dammit." He said it aloud to himself. And no, it wasn't his style to be engaged in combat and not fire a single return volley. Not his style to be pushed into a retreat unless it was strategic. But facts were facts, and he'd have to get creative pretty quick to turn this one around. And sometimes, he knew, even a big man loses a round.

He clipped the Uzi to his chest belt and gathered his gearbag onto his lap.

The dials continued rolling back down toward the small numbers. A couple of thunks rattled the craft and the instrument lights blinked simultaneously, flickered a moment, then went black altogether.

The airborne sharks to the rear were still at their machine guns, biting out little chunks here and there from the once-formidable warplane. A sudden bright flash erupted from under the wing of the lead jet, and he knew what it was. They had decided to speed his destruction with the air-to-air rocket.

Bolan gave the dying jet a hard yank around to the left and groped for the ejection-seat handle.

The numbers had fallen to zero.

It was now or never.

6

THE FIREBALL EXPLOSION lit up sky and ground alike. What had been an expensive workhorse warplane fell in flaming pieces. There was no time to mourn the disintegrated remains of the pilot, a good soldier and a good man.

Bolan, his chute not yet open, had less than a second of bright light with which to mentally photograph the terrain a few hundred feet below.

Only hundreds of feet away on the horizontal, and closing fast, one of the fighter planes roared toward him, its guns blinking out a code of cold-blooded finality as his chute opened.

The Executioner twisted the compact Uzi submachine gun to his left hip and tapped out a bloody code of his own. He buoyantly played with the forces of chaos unleashed in this patch of black sky and was aiming the curse-spitting Uzi at the flicker of reflected light he took to be the cockpit. The image of it was suspended in his perception. He was going for the vital signs in a frozen moment.

The Super Sabre screamed by within a few dozen feet of Bolan the sitting duck, its machine-gunned tracers still slicing through the night, even as the jet leaned over a quarter turn and disappeared in the blackness over the craggy top of a nearby plateau. There it was transformed into a flash-bright orange-and-red mushroom of broiling flames.

Bolan had no time to watch the light show, spectacular as it was. The turbulence from the plane's last pass was playing hell with the parachute, first nearly collapsing it, then flinging him around in the cords like some drunken marionette.

The chute lacked sufficient altitude to recover completely, and Bolan was dumped hard on the ground only a breath or two later. Hard, sure. Hard enough to spill the life out of a less seasoned man, and to come close in any case.

For several moments he stayed still where he had landed. He remained conscious, but the acute pain throbbing in his neck and spine was giving him cause to wonder whether that was such a blessing.

He took mental inventory. Bones intact, extremities in place and operative, no indications of any serious internal injuries. One of the remaining Super Sabres shrieked by overhead, then gave up the search and climbed away to join its already departing mate.

Bolan sat up and continued his inventory. He pulled the helmet off to examine a fresh cut on his forehead. The bleeding was already slowing. He pulled out a medical kit from the warbag, found a compress and firmly put it in place above his left eye.

Attention next moved to the hardware. The Uzi's muzzle had picked up a plug of badlands real estate, but otherwise was in order. On his knees, he partially dismantled the weapon by touch in the darkness, cleaned the barrel then quickly reassembled it.

The new Beretta was fine. It got a quick check and went back to leather with its silencer in place. Finally, the AutoMag. It, too, got a fast but thorough inspection and easily passed muster.

Bolan's next task was to get rid of the flight suit. He stashed it and the helmet beneath a large boulder, then piled some smaller rocks over them to complete the concealment.

Standing in his blacksuit, he stretched and shook out some of the aches collected during his landing phase.

He pulled the homing transponder out of its arm-side pocket and activated it, for what it was worth. It was a cinch to be useless there at the bottom of the canyon. He'd have to get it higher, and even then its range would be limited.

Looking around at the desolation of the place, Bolan realized it would be a miracle if anyone had any idea of where he was. He was far from sure himself. He briefly wondered about the jets dispatched from the carrier. No, they would probably not venture this far inland, if at all. Assuming his calculations were correct, Bolan's current position figured to be close to a hundred miles west of the shoreline.

A glance at his wrist chronometer showed midnight, Washington time. If there was to be a search at all, it would be in daylight. If and when a search party arrived, it would be interesting to see which side would send it.

They had seen him bail out. They had shot at him in his chute. They had briefly searched for him after he was on the ground. It was not hard to guess that they would be back.

Who were *they*?

At least Brognola would know that "Striker" was out of commission. He trusted the Stony Man team to do the right thing. Anna Charissa was the first priority, and the destruction of the vultures responsible a close second. Yeah, if necessary, Striker's fate must keep until that business was completed.

Sometimes he got the idea that Brognola and the

other Stony Man people considered him irreplaceable, like some kind of superman. But that was something Mack Bolan himself was careful not to believe. He was just a guy who saw a job that needed doing. The events of his life had granted him the proper training. And so he used that training and used it fully.

If Mack Bolan died tomorrow—or tonight—the job would still be there, needing to be done. Other men—Carl Lyons and Able Team, Katz and Phoenix Force—had seen the need and were already doing the work, in their own way, as he had: secretly, expecting no recognition for a task as humble as that of pure service to the living and their yet-unborn children.

The Executioner of the terrorist wars would survive. Maybe he, Mack Bolan, would not. Eventually, he certainly would not. But the Executioner would survive in some stony form, under some name, until the world was forever rid of the verminous animals that, although born as men, existed only to destroy mankind.

The cause was a hopeless one, utterly. Nothing less than the full commitment of good men to war everlasting versus evil was necessary to keep the sun shining even one more day.

He thought of Anna Charissa. What were her chances? What were the world's chances?

To the east, there were no mountains, just rocky terrain that led to forest and jungle, and beyond that lay miles and miles of marshland. There were almost no people living in this north central part of Nicaragua, nor for that matter anywhere beyond the Cordillera Isabella, the mountain range, that loomed fifty or sixty miles to the west.

If a man really wanted to be alone, this would be

the place. No large rivers here, not even roads linking the two coasts of a country that statistically had, in fact, one of the highest standards of living in all of Central America.

Far over the curve of the earth, he imagined, the night mist would be gathering to prepare the morning's fog. In some ways he was lucky, Bolan thought. There probably would be no fog in the morning in this place. Here the night was clear and starry, and the available light more than sufficient for picking out the dim pattern of low cliffs surrounding him on three sides. He picked out the tallest one and started climbing.

The mission had run into a temporary snag, he told himself. That lady would be recovered, somehow.

Yeah, somehow.

7

EVEN CLOSE UP she was a genuine beauty. Her features were strong yet delicate, suggestive of a cross between Sophia Loren and a young Cherokee maiden.

Anna Charissa carried her forty-three years more like thirty-three or thirty-four, young enough for smooth, clear skin, but mature enough for time to have softly etched a trace of character about her deep and timeless eyes.

Her beauty was evident in quiet abundance, but it did not stop at her skin. Anna's candor and intelligence had made her an international model of modern womanhood. Although completely nonmilitant in manner, her words and actions had always very clearly articulated the potential for peace in the world, and for the rights of humans to live in peace, free of torture.

Some said she would make as good a UN ambassador as her husband. If she somehow survived the hell she was currently enduring, that might yet come to be.

THE EVENTS OF THIS STRANGE DAY, earlier in Panama City and now here in God-knows-where, swirled through her mind, refusing to conform to any regular shape or fall into place in a meaningful pattern.

She tried again. They had flown into the country in midmorning and had received a polite, even pleasant welcome. Her husband, John Leonard Charissa, was not unknown to the Panamanians. In fact, he enjoyed great respect in that country for his contributions to Panama's prosperity in years past.

And Anna herself, if the truth be fully told, was possibly even more popular. She was aware of her celebrity status. In the early years of their marriage, she had been concerned that she not outshine her husband. John had been wonderful about that, however, and she need not have worried. He knew her concern and from the beginning had suggested that they work as a team, two people honestly dedicated to making a contribution to the planet. Neither of them cared as much for recognition as for their unique opportunity to make a difference.

So to Panama they had come, and their stated and actual purpose was solely goodwill, in whatever ways they could generate it.

At noon, both had spoken at a large state luncheon, followed by as many private conferences with important leaders as could be crammed into their public farewell address. Just prior to leaving for the airport, they had remarked on the success of their visit.

Then the world had cracked wide open with the sounds of automatic-weapons fire. They were pushed into the safety of an automobile. John Charissa's head had suddenly begun leaking red behind his left ear. Anna had moved to his side, trying to keep the wound closed with her hands. Then someone was pulling her off, dragging her away from her husband.

"You don't understand!" she had cried. "I must be with him!" She had thought the soldiers were American, so she could not understand why they were being so rough with her. They wore American uniforms. They took her to American helicopters.

But they were not Americans, and when she found out, it was too late to do anything—anything but fight, bite, kick and scream, all of which she did to the point where the ropes they had bound her with were bloodied from her raw wrists.

After what seemed hours in the helicopter, they had brought her to this place.

Her husband was dead, she told herself. What gain was there in believing otherwise if she was to effectively maintain her full energies at such a critical time, in such a critical situation? Her anger could be useful here; if properly managed, even a source of energy.

Not yet did she cry for her husband. She knew that the tears would come eventually, the inevitable cathartic expression of grief.

But she would not allow grief to weaken her yet. Later, but not now. For now, she would fight it. She felt the energy build within her as her anger boiled. Eventually, she knew, it would erupt.

The intensity of her massive anger in fact surprised her, even frightened her.

But she could not hate the animals that had slaughtered her husband in front of her eyes. Rage she could feel, yes. But not hatred. For her there was a distinction. Anger was honest and justified. Hatred was blind, destructive to all, especially to the one who harbored it.

Her capacity for compassion, even for criminals as ruthless as these, was unfathomable in its depth. For her, compassion did not imply feeling sorry for humanity. It was not the sugary nonsense that passed for compassion in so-called "polite" society.

No, it was the compassion that allowed for a solid punch in the mouth if that was necessary to set a person moving in the direction of the good path.

Anna Charissa could be one tough lady, as her captors had discovered in short order. Of the four men who had forced her into the helicopter earlier that afternoon, one of them now had two cracked ribs and a swollen left eye. Another had a broken thumb, and a third came back with a displaced kneecap. The fourth man had yet to stand up fully straight again as a result of an embarrassing groin hit delivered by her well-placed foot.

The blows had not gone unretaliated, however. She had ugly dark bruises on her forehead and right cheek. Her nobly chiseled chin was scuffed as a result of her being thrown head first onto the floor of the copter.

Oddly, the marks had little effect on her real beauty, as if the quality arose from within her, independent of such niceties as unblemished skin. Nor had the brutal treatment even slightly damaged her proud bearing.

Ropes bound her lacerated wrists, but she was okay now, having found righteous rage.

All she had to do was keep on top of it.

"PAY ATTENTION!" someone screamed at her.

The words came chopping out in a thick Spanish-flavored English.

"When I am giving you a signal, *señorita*, you will then speak that which you have been instructed to speak. *¿Entiende usted?* So, you will pay attention— or you will pay some other way, eh?"

The large khaki-dressed man stood directly in front of her. He stretched out his arm, letting his fingers admire the torn fabric of her clothing and the curving flesh beneath.

The man's covert intentions were not lost upon that good lady.

"Do what you will," she told him coldly. "I will not cooperate with the likes of you so-called men. Your evil lies will never echo from my mouth. Never. You are pigs!"

Red anger surged into the man's face.

"You *bitch!*" He raised his hand to slap her, but it did not happen.

Another man, smaller and darker, stood behind him and restrained his upstretched arm.

The small man spoke evenly. "It is not wise to do the *señorita* any further damage...it would show on the camera. The time for that will come soon enough, *sí?*" With that, he smiled and released his grip.

The larger man rubbed his wrist with his other hand and looked away momentarily. "*Sí*, but she *must* talk," he protested carefully. "Is that not the plan?"

"Then we change the plan," said the other, obviously the bigger man's superior in rank. The little man now stepped forward and faced her. His eyebrows arched as he drilled his dark gaze into hers.

He breathed the words into her face. "So, *señorita* does not wish to talk.... Very well. You will be gagged." The little man chuckled blackly.

"Heh-heh, that way you *cannot* talk," he laughed. "What do you say to that? Heh-heh-heh." While the man was enjoying himself, Anna Charissa drew on her fire, bared her teeth and lunged for the man's face.

But he had been expecting such a move. He stepped back easily, brushing away her attack.

Two guards immediately grabbed her and shoved her back into the chair with rough hands, then began lashing her to it.

"You disgust me," she snarled through gritted teeth. "You and your kind are the root of the evil in this world. And you will see. The world will not long tolerate your existence. You will see."

He laughed mockingly. "Yes, of course, we *will* see." He laughed demoniacally, then abruptly sobered and turned to one of the guards.

"Gag her," he snapped. Without waiting for the guards to comply, he turned and walked to the door, his eyes eerily aglow from some strange inner fire. A crooked smile rose to his lips, as if some hideous and entirely vengeful dream was about to come true.

He parted the makeshift curtain drawn over the rear door of the old transport plane and stood outside on its loading ramp. He put an American cigarette to his lips and lit it, cupping the flame against the sudden gust that materialized out of an otherwise still and starry night.

After a deep pull at the tobacco, he held the cigarette in front of his face and admired it. The Americans are good for some things, he mused, then stuck it back between his teeth and chuckled again. This time, he marveled at the beauty of his plan. Using Americans against the Americans.... Yes. That was beautiful.

He stood in the night coolness outside the transport plane, away from the hot bright lights that were necessary for the video cameras inside, and finished the smoke. After a moment he turned and leaned back inside the large cargo door.

"Pronto! Pronto!" he barked loudly to everyone.

"Time is moving quickly. Is the camera in position yet?"

"It is just one minute more, *comandante*," came the shouted reply.

The *comandante* smiled his dark smile and withdrew. Everything, of course, would occur on schedule because the penalty for failure was hideous torture, performed by others in the ranks, under his watchful direction. Neither the tortured nor his torturers enjoyed the ritual, and therefore there was great incentive not only to not screw up, but to keep others from screwing up, too. It also served to keep the tension level high and he preferred that.

The dark little man marched down the ramp and walked the few yards to the edge of the dirt airstrip.

Two technicians sat behind a jumbled array of portable video equipment spread out on a makeshift table. The makeshift outdoor "control room" featured several television monitors, a pair of recording decks, some audio equipment, even a very modest camera switcher console, plus other electronic paraphernalia. Wires and cables littered the ground, with one of the larger cables trailing out across a field toward a distant portable generator, its far-off placement necessary because of its noisy diesel combustion engine.

He walked over and wordlessly took a seat a few feet behind the table.

The technicians continued their work, fastening cable connectors and adjusting dials, occasionally murmuring something into their headphones.

A young soldier came running up and stopped in front of the little man.

"I am to tell you it is ready, *mi comandante*," he said, catching his breath.

The *comandante* smiled and waved the kid away. This, he reminded himself, was a very good thing he had going here. A sure thing.

Out on the strip, the C-130 transport's four big engines sputtered to life.

The *comandante*, a.k.a. Etalo Yareem, a.k.a. revolutionary, guerilla leader, terrorist—the little man of mixed blood and international parentage could now add another feather to his war hat. He could add "important television producer."

In a few hours, his little low-budget video program would make him world famous.

He liked that, liked it so much it brought a broad smile to his face. After all these years, he was very happy indeed.

Etalo Yareem had never heard of Mack Bolan.

Ignorance is bliss.

8

SUMMER WAS NEARING. Crickets repeatedly sawed away at the stillness surrounding Stony Man Farm, tirelessly performing their monotonous song as they had done for thousands, maybe millions of years.

Most people might associate the chirping critters with the peacefulness offered by the early-summer scene on this warm night.

Right now, however, most people were asleep and as oblivious as the Virginia crickets were to certain nocturnal shifts in events—events that could substantially alter the world in which they would awaken, come morning.

The lights were burning brightly long into the night at Stony Man Farm.

Hal Brognola hung up the phone. He had just finished talking with Jack Grimaldi. Their conversation had been brief.

Grimacing slightly, Brognola looked away from April's big eyes, not certain there was anything to be said.

April, too, was wordless. Unconsciously she raised her left thumb to her mouth and lightly pressed her teeth against its manicured nail.

"Whatever's happened," Brognola said at last, "Mack's seen worse."

The Fed reflexively reached into his pocket for another cigar. He gave up the search, remembering he had just smoked his last. Instead he paced to the window.

"You realize, Hal," April said, "that Mack would want us to put someone else on the Charissa mission. He might be angry to know we haven't done so yet. Don't get me wrong—I'm not at all suggesting that Mack is. . . is not okay. It's just that the deadline is real soon. We must act."

"Hell, I think I've considered it every which way," responded the weary Fed. "But we've got to consider our best use of resources. All our guys are good, and Grimaldi's been a godsend time after time. True, he's the logical choice to take over the mission. But he's also our best hope to recover Stony Man One on a timely basis, and our resources will be expanded by an order of magnitude at least."

So, okay, for the moment, all the eggs were in one basket. And if it didn't work, he admitted to himself, the consequences would be more than just a little egg on the face.

"Besides," he continued, "ultimately it's not us who call the shots. Our function is to provide support for Striker's lead. He's the boss and the prime weapon. Without him, all we have is good intentions."

Mack Bolan was indeed a spectacular demonstration of the difference that one man could make.

Then fifteen short minutes ago—no, make that fifteen *long* minutes ago—the world had begun disintegrating again. Devolution, some called it. Entropy. It was a force, in a way very much like gravity. Entropy, like gravity, had a purpose, had its good uses. Entropy was the warning sign that some essential foundation element was missing or eroding—or more accurately, that some guiding force or principle was not present.

Leo Turrin and Carl Lyons rushed into the War Room.

Aaron Kurtzman followed them and returned to his computer console against a side wall. He punched a few buttons before sitting down.

"Something's happened to Striker?" Carl asked, his hotshot manner belied by the direct, steady voice so familiar to Able Team.

Brognola looked over to Kurtzman at the computer. "You didn't tell them, Aaron?"

The computer whiz shook his head. "Thought you'd be best to do that," he muttered.

"Sit down, guys," the Fed began. "Thanks for being here, Carl, we are privileged to have you. This has just happened. Circumstantially, it looks bad. Striker's plane was being paced by unidentified aggressors when our radio connection terminated."

"Where was he?" asked Carl.

"Off Nicaragua. I just gave the coordinates to Grimaldi. Jack's—"

Lyons's eyes widened in surprise. "Nicaragua! Son of a— Hey, Hal, take a look at that printout there, the one on top." He laid a stack of computer printouts on the table in front of the chief White House liaison.

"Hal," said Turrin, "Carl and I think we've got something. We had the Agency pull some runs on that 'Yareem standard' thing Grimaldi picked up on—ran all the possible spelling variations, whatever. Then we ran it as a last name and, well, you've got it all right there in front of you."

"And," added Lyons, "the guy is Nicaraguan."

"Okay," said the Fed, glancing it over. "How does it lay out—are you talking about Striker's plane going down or about the Panama raid?"

"Maybe both," Able Team's former L.A. cop replied.

Brognola rubbed his neck. "Tell me something about this Nicaraguan."

Turrin took the lead. "The guy's name is Etalo Yareem, a small guy physically, about forty or so, from a commingling of nationalities. Heads a little-known guerilla band based in the Nicaraguan badlands—"

Brognola interrupted him. "You think Striker's jet stumbled too close?"

"It's a possibility," Carl came in. "Their base camp has never been located. There are many dissident factions operating down there, and quite a few of them hide out across the border to the north, in Honduras, then sweep back into the country to fight at night."

Turrin continued, with Lyons adding amplifying details. Yareem's organization had been in existence for many years, quite a while longer than Yareem had been part of it. The group kept a low, low profile. They had not been interested in making a name for themselves internationally. Historically, they had limited their activities to some occasional harassment within Nicaragua itself. After Yareem joined the group, word had it that he developed links with the Cubans, primarily for weapons.

"The Agency figures that Castro is just keeping the strings attached in case the Sandinistas get out of line, but other than that, the group has no true political purpose."

Hal Brognola gazed toward the ceiling. "So you figure that this guy is just Castro's ace in the hole?"

"That's the way it appears," said Leo.

"But we believe he's even more of an isolated phenomenon," said Carl.

"What do you mean by that?" asked Brognola.

"It's just a hunch," replied Leo, "but it won't go to sleep. Here, look at this Yareem character's background."

Leo pulled back the computer report and flipped through it, stopped after several pages.

"Yeah, here it is."

Turrin read aloud.

"At age twenty-six, Yareem was a soldier in the Nicaraguan national guard. He once discovered and defused a bomb in the general barracks, was later commended for his actions and promoted. There were persistent rumors, however, that Yareem had planted the bomb himself.

"A few years later he had been responsible for the arrest of nine unemployed men as Communist sympathizers. The Nicaraguan government at that time, unlike the present regime, was highly anti-Communist. The nine men were accused of treason and were swiftly executed by firing squad—the penalty prescribed by the *Codigo Militar*, the book of military law. More rumors followed, this time that Yareem had planted pro-Castro literature in the men's homes.

"Hal, the point is that this guy has a background of pulling stunts, especially the kind of stunts that get him attention from his superiors. From what I've been reading here, the Somozas caught on to his game. And he was probably not too popular with his own troops either. One of his men testified that Yareem had been in communication with the Cubans—that Yareem himself was a Communist sympathizer, and the evidence seemed to bear that out."

"Why didn't he get the firing squad, too?" asked April, who knew well the inevitability of seditious ambition and its heavy penalties.

"Yareem *was* scheduled to face the firing squad, the next morning in fact, but he escaped during the night," Lyons said.

"And a pretty bloody escape at that," injected Turrin. "Even some civilians died during it, but no need to go into all the details. He eventually stumbled on a band of thieves who lived a Gypsy life in the badlands. In time, the leader died and Yareem inherited his own little army."

"So," said Brognola, "you're saying that Yareem is acting on his own, hoping to get a rise out of Castro?" He sighed heavily. "Well, I prefer that to a direct Moscow-Havana plan."

The computer printer came to life at the far end of the room. April went over to read it as it spewed words onto paper.

"Bingo," she said. "Aaron has been checking on that Lear jet Jack followed out of Delaware. The registry is Colombian, owned by a farming conglomerate. And listen to this." She tore the sheet from the printer and returned to her chair. "The company's owner disappeared about two months ago. They found the body last week near his private airfield. The Lear had been missing since the man disappeared. The authorities had naturally assumed—et cetera, et cetera—ah! And guess who the dead man had recently been dealing with?"

Leo Turrin shot quick looks at Hal and Carl, then back at April Rose. "Not Etalo Yareem?"

"The same," she confirmed. "The Colombian authorities are asking us to supply them with any information we turn up as to the plane's or Yareem's whereabouts. They also suggest that Yareem is a very unpopular man in the underground there—the drug-traffic underground, that is.''

"Can I see that?" said Turrin.

She passed it over, and he read it carefully.

"More stunts, Hal," he reported. "He's been stinging big-time drug dealers. According to this, the guy should have big resources. He can buy any-thing—all kinds of mercenaries, all kinds of planes, choppers, pilots—fighter jets capable of downing an F-4 Phantom.''

"How far from the north central badlands was Striker at the time?" asked Lyons.

"About a hundred miles, we think," said Brog-nola.

"And when will Grimaldi reach the search area?"

"He's figuring to meet the carrier in a couple of hours. He'll refuel and be in the air by daybreak. There'll be navy search-and-rescue teams dispatched at the same time...."

He looked around the table at each of them. "Don't worry," he added. "We'll find him."

As soon as he said it, he wished he'd sounded more certain.

Hell, he wished he *was* more certain.

9

THE BADLANDS MOON HAD RISEN just after midnight.

None of its light, however, reached the western face where he climbed. Scaling the rough, nearly vertical cliff was especially treacherous in the near-total darkness. Finally, the black-on-black of the night slowly mutated into the indistinct shades of gray announcing the new day's dawn.

The going had been slow. Bolan had made only some two hundred vertical feet an hour, he figured, although the actual distance traveled along his necessarily zigzag route was probably many times the height of the cliff. Even the best and most adventuresome of mountaineers would not have attempted such a climb without spikes, ropes and a partner or two. Then again, most mountaineers climb for the thrill of the experience.

For Bolan, it was merely the latest at-hand task of a deadly serious job of survival—and victory.

The top proved to be a plateau, fairly wide along the north-facing side, which he had walked for some distance. Its depth was uncertain, concealed by a thick forest that began a hundred yards or so to the south and east.

In the clearing between the edge and the forest, the ground was undulated, pebbly in texture and marked by large rocks, occasional trees—some of them dead—and by patches of brush.

In the new light, something glinted beneath his foot, something man-made. He stooped to examine the object. It was a dial-face from an aircraft altimeter. He rubbed it in his hand and gave the plateau a second look.

Lying about two hundred yards from the edge, over a slight rise, was the main wreckage of the downed Super Sabre, smoldering still. Crossing to it, he passed other acrid fragments, burned and twisted, that were scattered about the area.

The morning air was still, deathly still, as he stepped toward the wreck. The ground crunched, even under his soft rubber-soled shoes. No birds sang in this desolate place.

Little remained of the former flying machine; at least not in any recognizable form. The same could be said of the plane's pilot as well, the only evidence being a blackened helmet frame with something charred inside. The helmet had a small hole near its right front edge, which Bolan figured had come from his Uzi the night before.

A distant sound grew from a faint buzz to a more familiar noise.

Helicopters.

Three of them. He could see them now, approaching from the north.

He pulled a scope from his pack for a closer look.

U.S. Army OH-6 Cayuse, combat-rigged. They were not quite a mile off, splitting up now, each taking a different direction.

His search party.

As he loaded the flare gun, a thought slipped through his mind, and he almost missed it. He brought it back to the fore, gave it his attention.

He would have guessed they'd be *Navy*.

From the carrier.

Yeah, not Army.

So far, the three choppers had been crisscrossing the low area, flying below the level of the plateau. It was a matter of minutes before they would be checking out the higher ground.

Bolan triggered the flare. It arced up into the clear morning sky.

It took only a moment for the helicopters to swallow the bait. One turned, then the other two, and all headed toward the plateau, regrouping along the way.

They were hooked now, for sure.

He left the edge of the cliff and tracked back to a tree near the jet wreckage. The tree was dead. He slipped his grip about the Uzi, primed it and made ready.

It was one hell of a weapon, the Uzi. Balancing perfectly in the big guy's right hand, the SMG weighed less than seven and a half pounds and was only seventeen inches in length from the tip of its short, snub barrel to the end of its folded metal stock. Each magazine clipped into its pistol grip held twenty-five rounds of high-velocity ammo. The ugly black handful of stamped steel could be fired easily from a one-hand hold, as Bolan had repeatedly demonstrated. Nine-millimeter copper-jacketed sizzlers came spitting out of the barrel at the rate of six hundred rounds a minute, each with a supersonic muzzle velocity of some 1,250 feet per second. Changing magazines took less than two seconds. Yeah, it was the kind of firepower that jungle fighter Mack Bolan appreciated.

It was the kind he could do with right now.

He watched as the helicopters regrouped.

On reaching the edge of the plateau, the copters split up again. The lead bird continued toward the Sabre's wreckage.

If the paint on the chopper was phony, it was a damn good job. Making a positive ID would have to be done the hard way. Bolan held the little submachine gun against the back of his thigh and stepped away from the tree to wave.

The little Cayuse came about and started to land. Some animated motion in the cockpit appeared to be an argument, a brief one. A gun turret rotated to Bolan's position.

There were a few things about the Cayuse that did not add up to "U.S. Army," not the least of which were the craft's ID numbers. Bolan compared them with the list he had memorized from the early reports of the Panama raid. Finding an exact match, he brought the Uzi's muzzle to bear on the cockpit and dispatched screaming death in that direction.

Sizzling slugs burned through Plexiglas and metal and tore into skin and bone, blasting blood onto the windows inside the hovering craft.

The copter fast-floated to the ground and bounced once on its skids, then tracked off, dragging the skids, and finally coming to rest a dozen feet farther on, basically intact. Its rotors continued whipping around.

Bolan was well within grenade-tossing distance, but the copter was too valuable.

He was sprinting toward it when the first challenger cracked open the rear door and poured out a hot stream of lead at the man in black.

The Executioner had already seen the door moving and had issued a few stuttering rounds of his own.

Then he dived to the ground and rolled into prone firing position to deliver the follow-up.

The challenger's missiles had plunked harmlessly into the gravel to Bolan's left, then ceased altogether. The follow-up rounds were unnecessary after all, and the blacksuited man held his fire, bounced to his feet and ducked under the rear of the idling copter.

The craft wobbled slightly, then a combat-booted foot appeared on the dirt next to the right-side skid. When the second foot came down, Bolan grabbed both of them and yanked the guy off his feet. The man fell to earth like a sack of cement, then lay there. The Executioner had expected more of a fight.

He dragged the hulk under the craft, turned him over and made a verification. Yeah, the guy was dead. The fallen bastard had come face to face with a rock when he met the ground.

Bolan crawled over the body and pulled himself to the front of the aircraft, then risked a peek through the lower windshield bubble and around the rudder pedals.

Both the pilot and copilot stared unblinkingly into eternity, their bloodied faces contorted in recognition of the end.

Suddenly, golfball-size holes began appearing in the windshield bubble, followed by the ricocheting crash of metal-on-metal throughout the cockpit. One of the other choppers had returned.

The noise of the Cayuse's still-whirring rotors had covered the new invader's approach. The man in black leaned inside the cockpit, his hands finding the machine-gun controls and manipulating them deftly while he squeezed into the seat and brought his eyes to the gunsight. A slight correction was all that was necessary. An instant later he watched the other pilot's hands leave the controls to clutch at his exploding heart.

The copilot snatched the controls, veering the other copter sharply up and away from the ground, then banked high into a turn and lined up for a return engagement.

Bolan abandoned the Cayuse and dashed for the cover of the dead tree. Halfway there he slowed. He made sure he was seen by the new challenger. It made no sense to draw any fire onto his ticket home.

It worked. The second copter shifted course slightly and came barreling down on that tree with everything it had.

The stream of 7.62mm screamers from an XM-27 pinned the Executioner facedown at the base of the steadily disintegrating tree. His right hand unclipped a grenade from his web belt. He primed it, waited until the chopper was almost on top of him, then lobbed it hard and high.

The HE arced up above the little helicopter and fell onto the main rotor blades. A dull *thunk* was followed almost instantaneously by a concussive explosion that ripped the rotors into splinters and collapsed the windshield bubble.

The force of the blast slammed the craft earthward, but before it hit, the Executioner's second grenade had sailed into the exposed cockpit. The new explosion split the chopper in two, touching off a fireball secondary, and finally leaving nothing but pieces, to rain in a phosphorous mist onto the plateau.

TWO DOWN, ONE TO GO. Bolan dragged the bodies from the Cayuse, latched all the doors and crawled into the pilot's seat. Everything was in order at the controls, despite numerous dents and holes nearby from the gunfire.

He goosed the throttle and twisted the main rotor pitch for takeoff. The little helicopter lifted off obediently. Not everything, however, turned out to be in order after all. The rudder pedals were useless, and the bird pinwheeled in circles over the same spot like a leaf in a whirlpool.

Trying the copilot pedals produced no improvement. Bolan reduced the pitch and floated the dizzying craft to the ground. The ground swayed as he stepped out of the helicopter, and his perceptions played tricks: his whole field of vision was spinning even though the ground was rock still. He fought a brief battle between his senses and his stomach. He kept his breath even and waited for the bout of dizziness to pass.

Recovered, he walked back to check the tail rotor. A bullet had severed a vital control line. Stepping back to the cockpit, alert for the enemy helicopter still unaccounted for, he flicked a few switches and shut down the engine.

As the rotors whined down, he began checking all the storage compartments, hoping to find a few tools.

There were no tools.

10

THE FORMER GREEN BERET'S IMAGE fuzzily took shape on the big video screen.

Sergeant Larry Shortner's fingers drummed on the tabletop as he read from the script lying in front of him.

He looked up at the camera only occasionally, but each look revealed increasing anxiety. It may have been tension, or maybe the bright lights, but a darkening frown dominated his features.

"Good morning, Mr. President," he began. "So far you have not complied with our demands. Perhaps you were waiting to find out what we meant when we said that something terrible will happen to Mrs. Charissa. That, as you will see, is most unfortunate, because something terrible has already begun happening to her.

"In case you do not believe what I say, we will show some pictures now. And then, sir, you will believe...and also comply with our demands, which we have increased. You will hear more about that after the pictures."

The TV picture rolled. A few glitches and some electronic snow passed across the screen. Then a new picture emerged. There was no sound portion in this segment, only an ever-present hissing.

In it, Anna Charissa appeared. The scene was inescapably the inside of a large transport plane. The camera remained locked into a stationary wide shot, providing a view facing rearward toward large cargo doors.

Seats were few, and the lady was seen being strapped into one of them. She was tied, feet and hands, and gagged with a scarf, probably the one she was wearing when she disappeared. A few small bruises on her face reflected the rough treatment she had received earlier, but otherwise she looked in reasonable health.

She did not, however, appear cooperative. It was plain that Anna Charissa was fighting her captors every step of the way. She kicked one of the men who was fastening her into the seat. The man responded by raising his open palm to slap her, but he restrained himself and returned to his task.

Two men wearing flight helmets entered the plane and walked past the camera into the unseen cockpit. They did not appear to be Americans.

Moments later the picture vibrated roughly, the result of engines starting up. The vibrations smoothed out quickly enough, but the picture remained slightly blurred. The men who had tied up the woman hurried to the rear of the plane and exited through the cargo doors, closing them as they deplaned.

The camera began shaking again. The picture quality was sufficient to see Anna being jostled in her seat. This continued for a long moment, then the picture broke up. More video glitches and snow passed briefly, followed by the reappearance of the same scene. The camera vibrated very little now.

One of the men from the cockpit walked into view. He passed Mrs. Charissa and lifted a canvas bundle from the wall several feet behind her. He slipped into the parachute's rigging and pulled the cinches tight.

Then he walked back to the rear of the plane and began opening the cargo doors. Daylight glared in.

Meanwhile, the second helmeted man entered the scene. He leaned over Anna Charissa and checked the bindings on her feet and arms. Satisfied, he donned a chute also and joined the other man at the rear. He looked back briefly toward the camera, then turned and tapped the first man on the shoulder. The first man made his jump.

At this point, Anna had twisted her head around to see them. Realizing what was happening, she turned back and looked wide-eyed into the camera, vigorously shaking her head back and forth.

"No! No!" She seemed to be screaming through the gag, but the continuous hissing was all that was heard.

At the rear door the remaining man cupped a hand to his mouth and shouted a few unheard words to the lady. Then he nodded curtly at the camera, turned and disappeared into the empty air.

Anna Charissa, alone on the plane, continued shaking her head for several seconds until her image disappeared. After more electronic interference, the picture again rolled and the unsmiling face of Sergeant Larry Shortner returned to the screen. The sound also resumed.

"As you now realize," he began in a humorless tone, "we are very sophisticated and our resources are many and great. Because you will waste valuable time trying to figure it out, we will tell you that the scene that you have just witnessed was recorded less than one hour ago.

"The pictures were relayed from the camera to our video recorder on the ground by a microwave transmitter aboard the plane. When I have finished what I have to say, this message will be sent, also by microwave, to a private receiving station set up in a hidden location in Mexico. It will be recorded on another videotape and anonymously delivered to the same Mexican television station that received our first message.

"Be assured that it will do you no good to look for the microwave receiver. First, because it will already be dismantled by the time you see this. Second, because you do not have time."

The former Green Beret looked down at this script, then continued. "And now, Mr. President, these are our wishes.

"Number one, the money that you are to deposit has been increased to two hundred fifty million in American dollars. Second, you, the American president, must appear on U.S. network television and tell the American people that capitalistic imperialism is responsible for world unrest and for the deaths of many people in Latin countries. Therefore, you will announce the withdrawal of American soldiers, including so-called 'advisers,' from all of Latin America.

"These demands must be met by twelve noon today, Washington time. According to our calculations, when you receive this message, you will have only hours to comply. Since both demands can be accomplished in one hour, then you will see that in fact we are being generous.

"As for what happens if you do not comply. . . . At exactly twelve noon, the plane carrying Mrs. Charissa will fall out of the sky and crash into your White House. And you, Mr. President, will have to explain to the world why *you* have killed her."

The screen went blank.

11

THE THIRD CHOPPER RETURNED, appearing suddenly, seemingly out of nowhere. It loomed up from below the northern edge of the plateau, less than a hundred yards from the disabled Cayuse.

Bolan quickly distanced himself from the crippled craft. He discharged a burst from the Uzi before diving for ground cover.

The new arrival settled its skids on the edge of the plateau while its pilot-gunner expertly pinned the Executioner behind a shallow rise in the terrain. Both back doors flew open and each discharged a soldier.

The two men spread out to either side of the craft, running in combat crouch and firing what appeared to be AK-47s.

Then, as quickly as it had appeared, the copter rose into the air and sank from sight below the cliff's edge. The whacking sound of its rotors faded.

Both men were running to widen their pincer advance. They fired as they ran. Neither took time to aim.

Bolan dashed to the lame copter as bullets kicked up dust on his heels. He leaped inside and flicked the switches that started the engine, then set the blade pitch on ''down'' and opened the throttle. Removing a packet of HE from his belt, he quickly placed it under the copilot chair and stuck a small radio receiver to it. Then, in almost the same motion, he was diving out the far-side door and rolling south in the whirling dust.

Counting on the dust cloud to cover his strategic retreat, he continued on to the rear, bouncing up into a running crouch and finally finding a rock large enough to squeeze behind.

The Uzi got a fresh clip installed as the first order of new business. That done, it was time to check out the results of the subterfuge.

The terrorist soldiers had begun closing the jaws of their two-pronged trap, concentrating their fire on the Cayuse. Both men swept in closer now, seeming to take confidence in the lack of return fire from the chopper. The helicopter was literally poked full of holes. Not a shard of plexi remained on the windshield.

One of the men brazened it out and stepped up to the pilot-side door, while his partner eased up near the rear door on the other side.

Bolan fingered the radio-controlled detonator switch and introduced them both to fiery hell.

The blast that boiled heavenward was suddenly shadowed by something that blocked out the sun for an instant, accompanied by a high-keening whistling sound. In less than a blink, two dark shapes flashed by overhead, the high whine doppling into crackling thunder.

Bolan knew what one of them was before he looked up. It was an AV-8B Harrier Vertical Take-off and Landing. One of Jack Grimaldi's favorite vehicles. The sight of it brought a brief smile of recognition to Bolan's lips.

Brief because two seconds behind the Harrier was another jet—one of the black Super Sabres from the night before.

The Sabre roared over him, guns blasting and tight

on the tail of the first plane, staying there even as the Harrier flipped into a tight high-banked turn and headed back into the rising sun at high speed.

Bolan heard the Sabre's pilot kick in his afterburner as he came out of the turn. The dark jet shot forward, gaining fast on the Harrier. And then a curious thing happened.

The Harrier stepped up and out of the Sabre's path, stopping in midair to wait for the black jet to whisk past. It was a very short wait.

Now the VTOL dropped and soared back up to speed. The pursuer had become the pursued.

This leap-frog technique, called VIFFing, or Vectoring In Forward Flight, was perfected by the U.S. Marine Corps pilots who discovered it. The Harrier was unique in this regard, much to the heart-stopping surprise of enemy pilots who had never heard of it. When the Harrier pilot "stepped out," he simply turned the thrust nozzles, which has the effect of reversing the jet's full power from forward to "antiforward" with an efficiency that blows ordinary air brakes right out of the sky.

The Sabre pilot had made two mistakes. The first was tangling with the Harrier at all. The second was in changing course, because when he did so, he lost the only advantage he had left—the morning sun shining into the Harrier pilot's eyes and, therefore, into his gunscope as well. The Sabre pilot did not live to regret it. In fact he did not live to complete his turn. The Harrier moved in easily now, blasting the black jet to so much flaming rain.

The Harrier steered clear of the exploding jet and steep-turned back toward Bolan. The deadly air dance had lasted less than forty seconds.

Bolan left his position, circled the burning remains of the Cayuse and made himself visible, all the while staying alert for the next appearance of the peek-a-boo chopper.

The "jump jet" pilot was indeed Jack Grimaldi. The fly guy picked a spot, put the VTOL into its hover mode and settled the bird to earth like a feather. Dust and gravel spewed away beneath its powerful jet thrusters. Bolan was forced to look away.

A moment later he was squeezing himself into the Harrier, a rare version modified to accommodate an additional occupant.

Except for a grin and a wave, Grimaldi dispensed with the formalities and immediately jumped the VTOL up into the air, then began rotating the thrusters for forward flight.

"You're a godsend, G-Force," Bolan said into the headset, once he had donned and adjusted the helmet. "You locked into my homer signal?"

"Not at first—I was out of range," replied the flier. "But me see lost brave's smoke signal plenty good, then me come like eagle."

"Jack, buddy, there's still another chopper around here. . . . Maybe you saw it on your way in."

"Roger, Sarge. I saw it okay, but it's not around here anymore. It headed north when the Sabre showed up."

"Jack, you short on fuel?"

"Negative."

"Then I don't understand why we're not tailing that copter. It'll lead us right to Anna Charissa."

"An hour ago you'd be right, Sarge, but Stony Man HQ reports the lady is en route to Washington."

"It's over?"

"Not over, boss," replied a grim Jack Grimaldi. "It's just begun."

12

"IT'S YOUR PLAY, SARGE. Even if we do catch up with that transport plane, we'd still have to figure out what the hell to do with it."

Grimaldi eased the power to full. The bird rose gracefully, seeking higher lanes for the long haul toward home.

"I'll call the Farm," Bolan muttered. "Hal know you got me yet?"

Grimaldi leveled out the Harrier at thirty thousand feet, made another slight course correction and set the trim.

"I told him I thought I saw you. He'd just finished figuring out how long it would take for me to intercept that transport carrying Anna Charissa. Even figured on two midair refuels, although I told him one might do it okay. I said I'd be risking a flame-out in this bird to try and hit Washington before 1100 hours, but I'd risk it anyway. Then when I told him about you, he was afraid we'd never be able to make up the time."

"How do you read it now, Jack—can we make it?"

"Betcher ass, buddy. 'Cept I don't know what the hell we're gonna do when we get there. Looks like they might want yours truly to pull the trigger."

"Shoot the lady down?"

"I will if I have to, Sarge, but I hate it."

"There's a way."

"You got something?"

"Negative," said Bolan. "But there's a way. We just got to think of it. How long we got?"

"Long ride, Sarge. Even at this speed, a coupla hours. I guess you know I didn't find your friend Latchford. The Agency thinks the V.V.A.A. is a front for a mercenary-recruitment operation. It ties in with a whole lot of guys, all of 'em vets, who've disappeared lately. Like Larry Shortner, the guy identified from the video message."

Bolan said nothing.

"I'm afraid Bobby Latchford fell into bad company, Mack. He's the enemy now. Right in this same damn game. I'm sorry, Sarge."

Bolan adjusted radio dials for satellite connection.

"Stony Man One here. Brief me, Hal."

"Good to hear your voice, Striker. What's your health, guy?"

"Intact."

"Great. Grimaldi fill you in?" asked Brognola.

"Yeah. What's the in-depth?"

"It's now coming up on 7:00 A.M. Five hours from now, at noon, a transport plane carrying Mrs. Charissa will—supposedly—collide with the White House. That much you know, I presume."

"Yeah."

"If the plane gets that far, we'll have to shoot it down. Mrs. Charissa would die in the crash anyway, if that's any consolation."

"You don't need me or Jack for that."

"No. . . ." The Fed's voice was hesitant.

"Then best if Jack and I circle back to the bad-lands and take out those guys behind this. We have a good idea where they're based."

"Well, maybe you're right. . . ."

"But?"

Brognola was silent.

"But," continued Bolan, speaking for the Fed, "since there's still time, you wonder if there's any other solution."

"I do," Hal admitted. "But quite frankly it doesn't matter whether the plane actually makes it to the White House or we down it—either way, we lose, they win."

"No."

As Bolan said it, the resolve behind the word echoed clear and forceful to the mountains surrounding Stony Man Farm.

The thought of terror winning this battle shuddered him to his soul. It banged up hard against the commitment residing within him, a solemn self-promise to defeat that mutant, Animal Man. The thought that held that commitment was never far from Bolan's consciousness, at no time more than a thought away. And every rethinking of it brought forth an infusion of power, a renewal of determination.

That infusion flowed through him now as he repeated the word to Brognola. "No. They will not win, Hal."

It seemed to take Brognola a moment to find his voice. "I can sense that," said the Fed, "but we're up against some very sophisticated creeps."

"Hal, couldn't there still be a pilot on the plane?"

"We scrambled fighters to intercept it when it entered U.S. airspace from the Gulf of Mexico," said Brognola.

"And?"

"They report no pilot visible, just a single passenger seen through a window in the fuselage. There aren't too many ports on that kind of plane, so I guess a hidden pilot is a possibility, but we lean toward it being computer-controlled from inside.''

''What about remote control?''

''The transmitter would have to be nearby, like in another plane, or there'd have to be a series of transmitters manned all along the route. So far we haven't located any second plane and the route-transmitters idea is out. April's got some information for you on the Yareem character, Mack. It seems we're dealing with one very smart fellow.''

April Rose brought the big guy up to date on the history of a madman.

13

ETALO YAREEM CONSIDERED HIMSELF a superior man in every way.

As he sat behind a dusty desk in the front room of the shack that was his office, he recounted the evidence of his brilliance.

First, there was this sizable and fortified encampment, virtually impregnable to surprise attack.

Then, within the camp were some of the best equipped fighting men that money and persuasion could buy. And there were a lot of them.

Best of all, however, was the plan. It was of his own devising, and it was foolproof. Faithful adherence to his own fanatical standard and a lot of dirty work was about to pay off. Already it had paid off to some degree. He now had the attention of the American president and very likely all of the American public, too. Very soon, he would have the attention of the world.

Yes, his brilliance would have the appreciation it so rightly deserved. No doubt he would be much in demand in high places. That would be pleasant, yes.

And so far everything had gone well.

His face soured. *Almost* everything had gone well.

A blot on perfection were those idiot mercenary pilots he had hired. They had no right to take matters into their own hands on the previous night. It was only by fate that they did not spoil the entire plan.

Even so, they had allowed the American pilot to escape, and that was not good.

But how could a single American be of any real danger to them? What could any Americans possibly do at this point? If they were thinking that the crash of Mrs. Charissa's plane would be the end of it, what a surprise it would be when they learned that it was just the beginning.

The front door burst open, shattering Yareem's daydream. The man who entered was a helicopter pilot. He stood only a few inches taller than Yareem, which is to say he was not tall. He stayed at the door, his hand still holding the handle, and struggled to catch his breath. *"Comandante,"* he gasped.

Yareem narrowed his eyes at the intruder. "Yes, Lieutenant?"

The intruder seemed to be having difficulty deciding how to communicate the message.

Yareem rose to his feet and leaned over his desk. "Say it, fool. Did your pilots find who parachuted last night? The American?"

The lieutenant looked mournful. "We found him, but he is gone. He has been picked up by one of his countrymen."

"A helicopter?"

"It was a jet, *comandante*. A fighter plane. One of our Sabres almost succeeded in shooting it down, but—"

"But? Are you saying we lost another of our jets?"

It took great courage for the man to speak the answer. "Yes, *comandante*. And two helicopters. The man who parachuted—he destroyed the helicopters."

"Alone? One man? Now tell me why you were not able to prevent this."

"The man—he was dressed in black—"

"Bah! You are an imbecile. How many men returned with you? I wish to speak to each one immediately."

The lieutenant's already ashen face whitened some more. Again he grasped the door handle to maintain his balance. "It is only myself. My copilot died shortly before I landed."

Etalo Yareem averted his eyes from the man as he walked around his desk and toward the door. Then he put his hand on the man's shoulder. "Lieutenant, it took great courage for you to come to me and report these things. I can admire that." He spoke the words softly, almost sincerely.

The other man's face reflected great confusion. Basically he wanted to run.

"Lieutenant," the terrorist leader continued gently, "please stand outside the door."

The puzzled man hesitated briefly, then turned and obeyed. A few feet beyond the doorway, he turned to face Yareem, who was standing in the doorframe and aiming his pistol at the failed pilot's head.

Yareem waited until the reality of the moment dawned on the man, perhaps a full second. Then he pulled the trigger and blew off the right half of the pilot's face.

The shot commanded the instant attention of a dozen terrorist soldiers working the area near the leader's shack. Yareem addressed them.

"This man," he shrilled, pointing at the corpse with his .45 automatic, "has failed to maintain the standard."

Saying no more, he spit on the body, holstered his weapon and disappeared back into his office, slamming the door in final punctuation of the statement.

Inside, he walked to his desk and sat down. Instantly he was back on his feet, pacing.

Worrying. He was very uneasy about this man in black who fought like an army. Perhaps he was one of those—what were they called—*penetration specialists*. If he was in Nicaragua, then perhaps the Americans already knew about Comandante Etalo Yareem and his encampment. Perhaps the Sabre pilots had taken the proper actions, after all, in shooting down this man's aircraft. Yes, perhaps they had actually prevented further penetration by a most dangerous man.

If the man knew what was good for him, he would stay away. This Yankee in black owed Yareem the lives of many men—how many? Fourteen, perhaps, if one counted the useless body lying outside the *comandante*'s office. He had also been responsible for the destruction of many valuable aircraft. Two jet fighters and two helicopters, a large percentage of the camp's little air force.

But there were yet other planes, other helicopters. And the most important plane was perfectly safe—and on its way to the American *casa blanca*, the White House.

It angered him beyond measure, nonetheless, this loss. He had risked his own life, for many months in Colombia, to acquire the things that he had.

There he had met many men who thought they were smart. Thought they were smarter than Etalo Yareem. If they were so smart, he laughed to himself, then why were they so dead now?

It was amazing what the American drug dealers would believe. Not that they are trusting individuals, no. But they are easily misled if one adopts the proper appearances: the right clothes, the right airplanes, the right words. The right connections also, of course.

His pacing had stopped. He indulged a chuckle. Lately, he had been finding much humor in his thoughts whenever they turned to the subject of the *americanos*.

The Americans thought they were always so right, and that was their weakness, he had decided. They wished to believe in their rightness, right to the end. So he had learned to allow them to think they were right. . . right to the end.

And they had so much greed for the material things. They thought these things by themselves brought power, but what did they know of real power? *Real power* commanded the destiny of nations. Money in itself was worthless unless one knew how to use it, as he did.

His money had been put to good use. It provided him with fine weapons, good jets, good helicopters, good fighting men. He had spent his money on the tools of power. With them, a man of brains such as himself could *make* power.

In a few hours, all of this would be proven. He was too smart to think the Americans would pay the ransom. Of course they would not, as any fool could guess. The ransom was beside the point, especially since the group's treasury was still quite healthy from his Colombian activities of some months ago. No, money was not a problem.

Some things were more powerful than money. Things that money could not buy. Like media exposure, which would soon be spreading word of Yareem's power. He was getting a hold on the strongest kind of power, that which came from men's minds. Once men came to *believe* that Etalo Yareem had power, then would he actually attain such power.

He was cackling openly now, alone in his office.

Through the window, he could see four of his soldiers removing the dead lieutenant's body.

Sudden rage filled him as he yanked open the door.

"Leave it there!" he screamed. "I want all of you to see what happens when the *standard is not met.*"

By the time he'd slammed the door and once again paced to his desk, the anger had subsided.

Then he remembered what had been so funny. Now his amusement overwhelmed him again. Wasn't it the Americans themselves who had taught him so much of what he was using to defeat them? Just as he had used the knowledge he gained from the Somozas to assist in their defeat.

The strange course a life can take, he mused. To think that the Somozas had sent him and others to the United States—at the Americans' invitation—to be trained in their ways of fighting...yes, that was quite funny as things had turned out.

And they had learned so much more than fighting. They had learned about *technology*. And they had learned about the American mind. Yareem had been a star pupil in that regard.

Especially, he had taken interest in TV. Now that was a very powerful thing indeed. With a few skilled technicians, it was easy to use. Americans believe what they see on TV. If one wished to make Americans believe, one got one's message on TV.

And so he had. Now they would believe.

Soon it would be time to make another TV message. He leaned up to his desk and found a blank piece of paper and a pencil. He propped his elbow on the desk and rested his head against his fist.

This was to be a very important message. This time, there must be proper mention of Fidel.

14

"SETTING NEW COURSE... zero-one-niner... Harrier out and surf's up."

Grimaldi dipped the jet's right wing in a smooth swift roll and eased the nose into a stiff dive.

There it was. The C-130 Hercules transport had just broken out of cloud and into the clear a few thousand feet below them. It wasn't alone. Four Air Force F-15 Eagles were pacing the big plane.

10:58. Too early for the world to know of the unfolding outrage. But late, late into the outrage itself.

The Harrier came down behind the fat transporter, gaining fast on its tail. One of the F-15's tipped its wings in recognition of the Harrier.

"Herky Bird's tailgate is wide open," said Grimaldi. "If that lady's in there, she'll be plenty cold. And she's lucky the plane's not flying any higher. Air's pretty thin up here."

"How close can we get, Jack?"

"You can see for yourself in approximately eleven seconds."

Grimaldi pulled the throttle back, easily at first, then more quickly. The shift against inertia was about four Gs.

Deftly, he had the nose up with two notches of flap activated to make it easier to pace the slower-moving C-130.

The end result was an eagle's-eye view of the transport's left side forty feet to the right of the Harrier.

The C-130 was probably twenty, possibly thirty years old, ancient by military standards. But it seemed to be in an adequate state of preservation.

Grimaldi inched the jet forward while Bolan checked out every inch of the transport with high-powered binoculars. Finally they eased abreast of the other plane's cockpit.

"Empty as a miser's heart," offered Grimaldi.

Bolan murmured blunt agreement.

"Flip side," he said.

On cue, the pilot briefly dipped down and under. Two seconds later they leveled out at a corresponding vantage point off the right side of the transport's big pug nose. Grimaldi slowed the Harrier to the relative crawl of the larger plane.

"There," growled Bolan.

Grimaldi held the jet even. "You see her?"

"Looks like. . . damn window's so small and dirty. I can make out the outline of a face, looks to be gagged with a red cloth, same color as the blouse. . . but her head's down. I haven't seen her move yet."

"Probably asleep from the thin air," said Grimaldi. "She's been in that seat for eight, maybe nine hours."

Jack waved to one of the chase-plane pilots. Momentarily the other flier's voice came through the radio.

"Howdy, Harrier. This is Eagle Team Leader. Over."

"Roger, Eagle Leader. Stony Bird here. Need your brief on this boat. Over."

"Will do, Stony Bird. Same as you're seeing. No pilot in evidence. Course is steady, true heading zero-one-niner, magnetic is zero-two-four. We picked her up coming off the Gulf past Key West. Airspeed unchanged. Altitude unchanged. ETA Washington 1200 hours. We are assigned to escort and monitor only. Can't figure this one out. Can you ease our curiosity? Over."

"Negative. Sorry, guy. Stony Bird out."

Grimaldi flicked a switch.

"You heard it, Sarge. We're finally here, but hell if I know what to do. You?"

It was a full moment before Mack Bolan replied.

"Jack, do you have any idea how long it would take to come up with a computer program to make the same flight you and I just made, from Nicaragua to D.C., taking into account all the variables like wind direction and velocity, isogonic variation, unforeseen weather conditions, other traffic, temperature differences?"

"From what I hear, Sarge, just about anything's possible these days."

"Yeah, well maybe. I've been thinking we're giving these guys a little too much credit. They flash us a few examples of high-tech and we're dazzled. Dazzled into believing they're a step ahead."

"I read you, guy. You think—"

"I think maybe we fell for standard propaganda dressed in new clothes. Let's say there's no computer controlling that plane. What does that leave us with—a hidden pilot? It's possible, but I doubt it. He'd have to go down with the plane and I don't think they've got a guy with balls like that. He sure isn't going to bail out just before it hits the White House. He'd never survive."

"What are you driving at, Sarge?"

"That the plan is not to crash the plane after all. They're smart enough to know we'd never let that

Herky Bird get anywhere near the White House. They *want* us to shoot it down.''

"No pilot and no computer," grunted Grimaldi. "Okay, what gives, then?"

"You see that thing that looks like a TV camera lens in the nose?"

Grimaldi eased the Harrier forward and lifted his visor for a better look. "No, I hadn't—but you're right. I see it."

The crisp environment of the upper atmosphere was charging Bolan's combat sense. His perceptions were razor sharp. War pursuit had put him in that place where remarkable things happen with the regularity of the everyday.

"That's remote control to another aircraft directly along the same lane," he said. "I'd bet on it."

"So far, air force hasn't found one." Grimaldi lowered his visor against the glare of the sun.

"No, maybe they can't," agreed the man behind him. "But I'm betting Jack Grimaldi can. . . ."

15

"There!" barked Bolan.

The hunch had paid off.

It was not the Lear jet he had spotted, but its black shadow whisking over the spring-brightened North Carolina terrain.

The Lear itself was practically invisible. It was an odd sight, a sleek business jet sporting nonreflective mottled camouflage colors.

It was a Gates Model 25. Rigorous scrutiny of the skies in search of everything that moved beyond Eagle Team's detection corridor had honed their eyes. Bolan could make out even small details on the plane's back.

But a lesser-trained eye might have looked directly at it a dozen times before the mind registered the fact. Outside of the camouflage factor, which rendered the Lear's outline indistinct, for the most part people tend to see only what they expect to see. Anything that exists outside the realm of the known and familiar tends to be automatically dismissed by the subconscious. One anthropologist has suggested that the Indians of the New World never saw the approach of Columbus's ships because such a sight would have been completely outside their realm of experience. The stimulus was never reported to the conscious mind and so remained "unseen."

In the normal course of affairs, one simply does not expect to see battle-dressed business jets.

The Lear's spectacular speed characteristics accounted for it not being spotted by the air force dragnet. It cruised well out of radio range of the transport for extended times, merely darting back to issue corrections via remote control.

As both the Lear and the C-130 neared Washington, however, their paths began of necessity to converge. They would eventually need more or less uninterrupted radio contact. As the transport began its descent into D.C., the Lear would have to gain altitude to keep the radio signal clear of the mountains. That would mean a line-of-sight relationship.

The C-130 was moving through western North Carolina and approaching the southwestern border of Virginia, while the Lear paced it from behind the Blue Ridge Mountains just to the west near the Tennessee border. The White House was some three hundred miles north-northeast. At the Herky Bird's cruising speed of 368 mph, it was less than an hour from its target. On schedule.

The radio crackled.

"Stony Bird, this is Eagle Leader."

"Go, Eagle," barked Grimaldi.

"That's a roger. We have descent in progress. We read it one-two-zero feet per minute. Over."

"Thanks, Eagle. Keep us posted. Stony Bird out."

"Jack," said Bolan, "we must have a word with our friends in the Lear. Fast."

But Grimaldi was already veering the Harrier in a steep power dive in the appointed direction, swinging around slightly to come in dead on the Lear's six o'clock. It took a dozen seconds.

The Harrier was abreast of the Lear with such suddenness that Bolan could read the look of surprise on the Lear jockey's face without the need of binoculars.

Grimaldi, for his part, stared sternly into the Lear guy's eyes and delivered a brusque thumbs-down gesture like a skyborne motorcycle cop motioning a highway jerk to pull over. Grimaldi pointed to a deserted blacktop road below that separated two large tobacco fields.

The Lear pilot raised a .45 automatic with his right hand and waved it at them while shaking his head at the same time. Then he put down the gun and returned his right hand into view. With it, he flashed them the international one-finger signal for "get screwed."

The geography below was sparsely populated, mostly farmland in the flat areas, forested low mountains in others, with lush shades of green pervading both.

The guys in the Lear believed that no one would be stupid enough to shoot at them. Mack Bolan decided it would be a good idea to put some doubt into their equation.

He instructed Jack to demonstrate some firepower, as harmlessly as possible. . . .

Grimaldi peeled off to the left and positioned himself for a run directly at the Lear. Coming in at a forty-five-degree angle, he picked his spot carefully and delivered a short volley of hot lead across the nose of the Lear. The machine-gun bullets were followed instantly by the Harrier itself, whipping close over the top of the other jet.

Grimaldi returned the Harrier to its place side-by-side with the Lear.

This time they ignored him, refusing even to look in his direction.

"Son of a bitch," muttered Grimaldi. "Hold on, Sarge. This could backfire."

"Do what you gotta," said the Executioner.

Grimaldi glided closer until wing nearly touched wing, then positioned the Harrier's right wing tip under the tip tank of the Lear's left wing. When the distance was within inches, Grimaldi did something very dangerous to the structure of his own wing. He snapped his plane into a fast quarter roll, giving the Lear a sharp tap in the process.

As Grimaldi steered clear, the Lear dipped to the right. The Lear pilot fought the controls, grossly over-corrected, and the camouflaged business jet dived hard to the left, momentarily out of control. Then the pilot got himself together and peeled off fast to the right again, apparently deciding to get the hell out.

The Lear 25 is a superior flying machine, but its maneuverability pales next to the Harrier. And Jack Grimaldi was possessed of some seventh sense that enabled him to anticipate every move the terrorist pilot tried.

Escape for the Lear was impossible. Within seconds, Grimaldi had the Harrier floating off the Lear's left side again. The fly guy now repeated his thumbs-down cop gesture.

This time it worked. The Lear pulled out a notch of flaps and began a slow circling descent to the highway.

The Lear pilot was about to lose his license.

For good.

11:14 A.M. Forty-six minutes remained. Although the C-130 was still on a collision course with the White House, enough time was left. *If* . . . .

If the Lear did indeed contain the remote-control device.

If it could be operated from here, or quickly moved within range.

If there were no other surprises, like maybe a remote-detonation switch, or a timed explosive in the transport, or some other failsafe device....

"Stony Bird, Stony Bird, this is Eagle Leader. Do you read? Acknowledge."

"This is Stony Bird," replied Grimaldi. "Go ahead, Eagle."

"Rate of descent moving up now, to two-five-zero. I repeat, that is 250 feet per minute. Eagle over."

"Gotcha, Eagle Leader. Stony Bird out."

"It's the Lear," said Bolan. "They're doing it on purpose to rattle us off their hides. If they don't touch down in ten seconds...." He paused to consider the consequences. "Then we blast it."

The C-130 hadn't been all that high above the peaks to begin with. And now.... It was an image Bolan preferred not to entertain, an image of a good lady scattered across a mountaintop. Time was measured now in the heartbeat dimension.

Ahead of them, the camouflaged jet touched down and rolled along the highway for an increasingly hazardous distance. Finally the brakes locked and the plane skidded, slewing to a halt just short of a shallow crest in the roadway. Its right landing gear touched the edge of the asphalt shoulder.

Unlike the Lear, the Harrier needed no highway to land.

As Grimaldi lowered the plane toward the ground about twenty yards behind the war-painted Lear, he had Bolan's voice in his ear.

"My game down here, Jack. Just drop me and go back up, keep that lady company."

As the undergear touched ground, Bolan was out and down and back in his own element, back on his primary domain: Earth.

He ran toward the other plane in a low crouch, lifting the AutoMag out of its holster and shifting it to his left hand, then pulling up the Uzi into a useful position in his right.

He did not see Grimaldi take off, just heard the screaming whine, deafening at first, fade up into the sky behind him.

The noise was replaced by the shrill idle of the Lear's engines.

Some movement was evident through the Lear's little portholes. The pilot had left the controls. Bolan counted three terrorists, but had to assume more than that. The sleek jet could seat twelve.

He made the ditch at the edge of the blacktop, took the last few feet in a headlong dive and rolled up into shooting position: a single smooth motion.

The wings wobbled momentarily, indicating frantic movement inside the craft. Window curtains were being hastily drawn, one after another.

The top half of the jet's two-piece door opened slowly, hinged from the top of the fuselage. The bottom half swung out and down as it was transformed into its function as boarding ramp.

A rifle came suddenly flying out and clattered onto the blacktop. It was followed by a man in khaki, who carefully stepped out with hands above his head. He was shouting something, probably "Don't shoot," but the engines muted it to nothing.

The silently moving lips were followed closely, however, by a sound that could be heard. The loud

JOIN FORCES WITH THE EXECUTIONER AND HIS NEW AVENGERS!

THE EXECUTIONER

MACK BOLAN LIVES
IN EXPLOSIVE ALL-

He learned his deadly skills in Vietnam…then put them to good use by destroying the Mafia in a blazing one-man war. Now **Mack Bolan** is back to battl new threats to freedom—and he's recruited some high-powered avengers to help…**Able Team**—Bolan's famous Death Squad from Vietnam—now reborn to tackle urban savagery too vicious for regular law enforcement. And **Phoenix Force**—five extraordinary warriors handpicked by Bolan to fight the dirtiest of anti-terrorist wars around the world.

In the forefront is Mack Bolan himself, the Executioner, waging his single-handed war on the enemies of justice and democracy wherever they hide.

Fight alongside these three courageous forces for freedom in all-new, pulse-pounding action-adventure novels! Travel to the jungles of South America, the scorching sands of the Sahara desert, and the desolate mountains of Turkey. And feel the pressure and excitement building page after page, with non-stop action that keeps you enthralled until the explosive conclusion! Yes, Mack Bolan and his avengers are living large…and they'll fight against all odds to protect our way of life!

Now you can have all the new Executioner novels delivered right to your home!

You won't want to miss a single one of these exciting new action-adventures. And you don't have to! Just fill out and mail the card at right, and we'll enter your name in the Executioner home subscription plan. You'll then receive four brand-new action-packed books in the Executioner series every other month, delivered right to your home! You'll get two **Mack Bolan** novels, one **Able Team** book and one **Phoenix Force**. No need to worry about sellouts at the bookstore…you'll receive the latest books by mail as soon as they come off the presses. That's four enthralling action novels every other month, featuring all three of the exciting series included in the Executioner library. Mail the card today to start your adventure.

FREE! Mack Bolan bumper sticker.

When we receive your card we'll send your four explosive Executioner novels and, absolutely FREE, a Mack Bolan "Live Large" bumper sticker! This large, colorful bumper sticker will look great on your car, your bulletin board, or anywhere else you want people to know that you like to "live large." And you are under no obligation to buy anything—because your first four books come on a 10-day free trial! If you're not thrilled with these four exciting books, just return them to us and you'll owe nothing. The bumper sticker is yours to keep, FREE!

Don't miss a single one of these thrilling novels…mail the card now, while you're thinking about it. And get the Mack Bolan bumper sticker FREE as our gift!

LARGER THAN EVER NEW ADVENTURES!

FREE! MACK BOLAN BUMPER STICKER
when you join our home subscription plan.

Gold Eagle Reader Service, a Division of Worldwide Libraries
649 Ontario Street, Stratford, Ontario N5A 6W2

YES, please send me my first four Executioner novels, and include my FREE Mack Bolan bumper sticker as a gift. These first four books are mine to examine free for 10 days. If I am not entirely satisfied with these books, I will return them within 10 days and owe nothing. If I decide to keep these novels, I will pay just $1.95 per book (total $7.80). I will then receive the four new Executioner novels every other month as soon as they come off the presses, and will be billed the same low price of $7.80 per shipment. I understand that each shipment will contain two Mack Bolan novels, one Able Team and one Phoenix Force. There are no shipping and handling or any other hidden charges. I may cancel this arrangement at any time, and the bumper sticker is mine to keep as a FREE gift, even if I do not buy any additional books.

404-CIM-7AAE

Name	(please print)	
Address		Apt No.
City	Province	Postal Code
Signature	(If under 18, parent or guardian must sign.)	

This offer limited to one order per household. We reserve the right to exercise discretion in granting membership. If price changes are necessary, you will be notified. Offer expires September 30, 1983.

PRINTED IN CANADA

popping noises coincided with a series of sparks flashing from within the darkened cabin area.

The descending man's body suddenly jerked forward off the ladder and came tumbling down face first onto the hot hard pavement, coming to rest in a tangled heap at the foot of the steps. Neck, arms and legs were askew like a crash-landed vulture.

Before the dead man had touched the ground, however, the Executioner's response was sizzling from the AutoMag at the source of the sparks. The sparks stopped. The plane shook from the force of the guy's body slamming back into the far-side cabin wall.

Two down. At least one more to go.

Bolan checked the time. 11:23.

Thirty-seven minutes.

The Lear whined. The sun, directly overhead, was hot now.

The plane was still wobbling when Bolan made his move, digging out of the ditch and rolling under the near wing. From there he fast-crawled to the fuselage underbody.

From a crouch beneath the Lear, he guessed where the edge of the plane's interior floor began and put his ear to the body just above that point.

It took him a moment to tune out the pervasive vibration of the idling engines.

Ten seconds of no sound or movement inside the plane was the optimum that could be invested. He used his watch to check them off. Combat can distort a man's sense of time; there were times to trust one's own inner clock and times not to: this was in the latter category.

He moved, creeping to a position forward of the door, then scanned the floor inside toward the rear.

A bleeding body lay crumpled backward across a pair of seats. The guy's chattergun was lying harmlessly in the aisle.

The back-up choppers were landing now, two hundred feet away. Bolan noticed them peripherally. There were four, each discharging a large group of armed men wearing fatigues and helmets.

Bolan did not wait for them. Very smoothly he eased himself into the hatchway and looked left toward the flight deck. There was a gun there, a .45 automatic. It was attached to a hand and the hand, in turn, attached to a body. A dead body.

It was the pilot. Bolan crawled up to the body, confirmed it as dead, then moved over it and continued forward.

The cockpit was empty.

Bolan stepped back to the pilot's body and tried to put the pieces together. It was, he decided, a murder-suicide. The suicide was the pilot.

The murder was Anna Charissa's. Or soon would be.

The pilot, before taking his own life, had fired several shots into a plywood panel encrusted with lights, dials and switches that had been crudely, but adequately, installed in place of the copilot's control yoke.

It was the remote-control device for the lady's transport plane.

16

IN RESPONSE to its faint, insistent beeping, Bolan pulled the microradio from its sleeve pocket and acknowledged bluntly: "Yeah."

"Stony Bird here, Sarge—"

The toneless microspeaker did not mask the urgency in Jack Grimaldi's voice.

"I don't want to panic you, man," continued the flier, "but about two minutes ago the transport started pulling some strange maneuvers. . . ."

"Like what?"

"The thing was losing altitude when I got here, but then it suddenly started a steep climb to starboard under full power—I thought for sure it was gonna stall any second, but then it rolls over into a hard port. Next thing I know, it levels off. Well, almost levels off—it's still leaning port a little. Now the power comes way back."

"What do you anticipate?"

"The thing's falling out of the sky, Sarge, and the sky ain't too high in these parts on account of the mountains here."

"Read that timewise for me."

"That's a tough call. Could be two, three minutes, depending. Or maybe ten or twelve minutes, tops. With luck, that is—you got any?"

Bolan ducked back into the Lear's flight deck, squeezed himself into the copilot chair and scanned the butchered remote-control panel. His fingers found a small joystick and pushed it a few degrees to the right.

"How's it look now?" he asked the Harrier pilot. "Any change?"

"Nah."

Bolan pushed the stick the rest of the way. "Now?"

"Negative. You at the RC?"

"What's left of it."

"What happened?"

"Guy shot it," growled Bolan, something in him strongly wishing the pilot who had controlled somebody else's fate from this seat were still alive. So he could die again.

The backup crews had the plane surrounded. Bolan heard someone bark through a megaphone.

"Stay tuned, Jack. I'll be back at you."

He slipped the radio back into its place, leaned over and flipped a pair of switches on the Lear's regular instrument panel. The power quit, and the twin jet engines began their long whining wind-down.

Outside, the megaphone voice was clearer. When he heard what it was saying, he smiled at the irony.

He walked back toward the doorway, bending once to pick up the dead pilot's .45. When he reached the opening, he tossed the pistol through it and out onto the blacktop. Then he removed his own weapons and stowed them on the nearest seat.

The Executioner clasped his hands together as if to pray, then moved them to the top of his head and stepped out onto the first step.

"Ver-r-ry slowly," warned the megaphone.

On reaching the last step, two soldiers sprang from beneath the plane and roughly grabbed an arm each.

Bolan did not resist. This was the kind of thing that he would have avoided like the last plague in hell, back in the Mafia war.

Two more men broke cover and ran toward him.

"Hey, cool it!" shouted one of the runners. "That's our guy."

"Do not interfere!" insisted the megaphone.

"Go to hell," said Herman "Gadgets" Schwarz, reaching Bolan and shooing away the men holding him. "Hi, Sarge," he said quietly.

A few feet behind him, the second man stopped, turned toward the megaphone guy and waved both arms. It was Rosario "Pol" Blancanales. He and Schwarz, the electronics genius and gadget man, worked together as part of Stony Man's crack Able Team.

"It's okay," shouted Blancanales. "It's Colonel Phoenix...Army."

A slight pause was followed by amplified regrets. "Our apologies, Colonel," said the megaphone.

Bolan wasted no time on greetings.

"Gadgets, you bring your gear?"

"What ain't here," he said, pointing to a fabric satchel slung from his shoulder, "is in the chopper."

Bolan checked his watch.

11:34.

He turned and legged it into the plane. The other two, needing no signal, followed.

Schwarz saw the battered RC panel. "Aw, shit," he groaned.

"I know *that*," said Bolan, "but can you fix it—"

"Of course I can fix it."

"—in less than ten minutes?"

Schwarz frowned. "Damn thing's ancient, way before solid state."

The electronics wizard slid into the copilot seat and pulled a pair of screwdrivers from his satchel. "I'd say it's from an old Firebee 124—a Teledyne Ryan target drone, turbojet-powered. 'Course, the plywood's a more recent feature, probably so they could fit it in here...."

Bolan placed his hand firmly on Gadgets's shoulder. "Thanks, buddy. I knew you'd come through. You, too, Pol." He momentarily stepped away from the cockpit passageway to allow Blancanales room to squeeze by and crawl into the pilot chair.

Schwarz handed Blancanales a screwdriver. "You take that side. Let's get this thing outa here."

"Oh-oh," said Blancanales, stopping cold. "I don't like the looks of this."

"What the hell do you know about electronics?" said Schwarz, feigning annoyance.

"I mean the *español*." The older man pointed with the screwdriver. "See the Spanish names next to each of these switches?"

"*Sí,*" said Schwarz.

"This switch has part of its label missing because of the bullethole." He tapped it with his finger. "But its full meaning is *activate time bomb*."

Bolan broke the silence first. "What's the position of the switch—on or off?"

"On," Pol said, "or at least it conforms with the others that are."

Gadgets's side of the panel was loose now. He reached behind it and began snipping off wires.

"That's the switch I'll work on first," he said. "Don't know if it'll do any good, though. When you build a time bomb, you don't generally make any provision to stop it—you don't normally plan on changing your mind."

"Twelve noon," said Bolan, mostly to himself.

"I know, I know," muttered Gadgets.

"The terrorists set it for noon," continued Bolan, brooding. "They would have known there'd be a high risk of missing the primary target. . . and they'd want the world to think we shot it down and the lady with it. Even if we didn't."

Heat radiated from the southern blacktop road that surrounded them. The overhead sun blazed into the cockpit.

11:41.

Faint beeping sounds came from within his sleeve pocket. He pulled out the microradio and acknowledged.

"Stony Bird here," came back the thin, tinny reply.

"I read, Jack, but not loud and clear. How far away are you?"

"Plenty. She's making one big lazy circle out here. Missed one of the Blue Ridge peaks by a couple hundred feet on the last pass, so the next one *is* the last pass. We got real lucky this time. The Hercules approached on the windward side—if it had been the *lee*, well, it'd be all over by now."

"Okay, buddy, what kind of numbers can you give us—worst possible, down and dirty."

"Best is twelve, maybe thirteen. Worst is eleven, maybe ten minutes. Maybe less."

"There!" said Schwarz, lifting the panel that held the Teledyne workings clear of its moorings.

"Later, Jack." Bolan tucked the radio away, looked hard at Schwarz.

"Gadgets, buddy, if there's a way you can fix that thing right here, I'll get the Lear in the air and start closing the gap. We got a definite range problem."

Schwarz hefted the bulky panel and tucked it under his arm. "I agree with you on the range problem, but take a look at the floor here. That black stuff is hydraulic fluid. Here, watch this."

The gadget man reached over to the pilot's yoke and swiveled the controls back and forth. "Look at the wings. You see any ailerons moving?"

Bolan moved back a few steps and leaned out the door. "Got it, buddy. Let's git."

The two guys from Able Team scrambled out of the cockpit, stepping nimbly over the corpse of the terrorist pilot still bleeding on the aisle floor of the passenger section.

The Executioner scooped up his weapons and was gone.

17

JACK GRIMALDI'S IDEA OF HELL was where a guy had to sit and wait for the rest of eternity, feeling helpless and hopeless.

On the other hand, his idea of heaven was being able to wing solo through the skies in advanced state-of-the art aircraft like the AV-8B Harrier.

He thought it odd, therefore, that life could be so paradoxical as to serve up large portions of hell while he was sitting at heaven's very table.

Grimaldi loved his job. Over-all he couldn't imagine a better thing to be doing with his life. But that did not mean he loved every moment of it, and he especially did not like waiting.

A mere few hundred feet from him, a life was at stake, completely out of reach. Each minute that passed brought that life closer to its final moment. And there was nothing he could do but sit in the sky and *wait*.

He had never met Anna Charissa and, in the normal course of events, might never have expected to. Indeed, he still might not.

But he had seen her on television and there was no doubt about it. She was an extraordinary woman. It wasn't just her physical beauty that had made him take notice, though that was what first attracted his attention. It was something about her eyes, something that reflected an inner quality.

He felt responsible for her. And all he could do was sit and wait. And watch.

The C-130 was steadily descending. Normally, at its present rate of descent from seven thousand feet, its shallow spiral to reach sea level would take awhile. Unfortunately, there was more than air between it and sea level. There were mountains. At least one of those mountains was over six thousand feet high.

Grimaldi was no stranger to the high ground, in one form or another. The high ground, so to speak, was where the big boys played, for the high stakes. The ante up here was the price of your life. Winners were different people than losers. Winners did not plan to win only half the time, depending on the luck of the draw. Winners operated according to the principle that how a particular card was played was as important, often more important, than the card itself.

Grimaldi pondered the cards in his hand at this sky-high table and tried to make them into something—anything...a straight, a flush, hell even a pair of deuces. The call was coming round the table toward him. Where was that ace he needed?

But he *did* have an ace. If Mack Bolan was handling the business on the ground, then the business was getting handled. Period. Jack knew well that the big guy never let anybody down. That is, unless they had it coming, and then it was not a let down, it was a stomp-down to six feet under.

Which was where Grimaldi figured he'd be if he had not jumped at the chance to enroll in Mack Bolan's school of thought-in-action. Jack Grimaldi had been a different kind of hotshot back then, running airborne errands for the Mafia. The way he figured it now, he'd been blind before he met Bolan. He hadn't seen what a dead-end job he was in. It took the Executioner himself to bring him to his senses. The Sarge had pointed out that in the Mafia, *all* the jobs were dead end.

The true test of a man's character does not even begin until he's laid bare the horrifying emptiness behind the trappings. And that's what they were; the money, the free time, the easy broads—trappings.

Turning coat on the "organization" was a story few living lips could tell. Grimaldi had a lot to be thankful for. Tough moments like this one were a small price indeed, no matter how hellish. Times like this demanded everything he had inside and, yes, he knew he could take it, could fight not just to survive, but to survive and prevail.

The C-130 suddenly dropped several hundred feet. Just as quickly, it recovered and ascended slightly, almost back to the Harrier's level.

Grimaldi flicked on the radio. "Hey, Sarge, what the hell's going on down there?"

A steady voice replied. "Gadgets is going at it hot and heavy, guy. Start looking for a place to set the lady down."

"Not anywhere around here, boss. What ain't mountains is hills. We'd better aim for Pope AFB. That's way over near Fayetteville."

"How far from you, Jack?"

"Maybe twenty miles."

"In minutes."

"Seven or eight at least, but right now the damn thing's heading in the opposite direction."

On a collision course with the Blue Ridge Mountains. . . .

THE FAMILIAR-LOOKING Bell UH-1H Iroquois, better known as the Huey, has earned a brilliant record for usefulness in combat and utility. Despite that, however, the large chopper is decidedly on the slow side, with a maximum rated speed of just 127 mph.

The Huey that carried Mack Bolan and his brother warriors was pushing that maximum as it skimmed over the hills and ridges of North Carolina. While Pol Blancanales took up the copilot position in front, Bolan and Schwarz worked on the remote-control device in the aft cargo section.

Their pilot was a sharp young army lieutenant Bolan had never met before. The young officer knew his business well and kept the ride smooth for the delicate work going on in the rear.

"Better tell 'em to start foaming the runway at Pope," Schwarz called to the pilot. He wiped the sweat from his forehead, looked over at Bolan. "There's no switch here for landing gear. That means a belly job. How much time we got?"

"Less than a minute to clear a mountain, buddy, otherwise the foam won't be much use."

Gadgets shifted the bulky panel around to face Bolan. "You can get set now. Pol can read you which switch is which." He reached over the panel and adjusted several of the knobs and switches. "This way," he continued, "she's all set to climb like hell as soon as we reattach full power."

Blancanales handed Bolan the copilot headset and Bolan put it on. These guys are something else, he thought. If there had been time, he might have let himself be overwhelmed at their dedication to supporting him. But there was no time for anything but the job at hand.

Grimaldi's voice sliced through the headset. "Listen, Sarge, it's gonna hit for sure. I can't hope anymore, and I don't wanna watch either."

It was a tense, dense moment before the flyboy continued. "Hey, that was *close*. The updraft just pulled her over, but she's headed down fast on the other side. Holy...."

There was another, longer pause.

"She's climbing out! I don't believe it. Hey, you did it! You guys got that thing working!"

Out of the corner of his eye, Bolan saw Gadgets Schwarz lean back against a bulkhead and release a long, hard sigh.

"Yeah, Jack," muttered Bolan. "It's going. Tell me where to point it."

"Well, *all right*!" shouted Grimaldi. "I need a stiff bank to port, forty-five degrees...three, two—*now!*"

Bolan moved the small joystick a few careful degrees to the left.

"Get the nose up! Get the nose—okay, that's good."

Mack Bolan had done many things in his hard life that he could not have predicted. Now he had another item to add to a growing list: flying an airplane he could not see.

But he had Jack Grimaldi for eyes.

Jack was back in his ear. "You're lookin' good, Sarge. Start straightening her out...easy, easy...she needs some right rudder—whoa! A little less...there ya go."

The Executioner checked the time.

11:53.

Seven minutes.

"Jack," said Bolan. "Can you see us yet?"

"Negative. You'll see the base before you see the lady and me."

"We need her on the ground by twelve noon, guy. Can she make it?"

"How come noon? I thought that was just for the White House."

Bolan told him about the time bomb.

"Aw, *hell*...just when I thought we was already heroes. Hey, time to cut the power back...not all the way, just about forty percent...and give us some flaps—first notch."

Bolan's blue eyes searched the panel.

"Uh-oh. No flaps," he grunted.

"Mother of...." Grimaldi's voice trailed off into an angry litany.

"Keep an eye on the nose, Jack. I'm pulling it up."

"Better power back then, another twenty percent," said the Harrier pilot. "Wait. Bring the nose back down a little...little more—good. Hold it there."

"The field's coming up, Mack," reported Pol Blancanales.

The east-west runway was foamed. Emergency equipment stood by.

"Give her a shallow bank to starboard, Sarge. That'll put us on base leg."

"There she is!" shouted Blancanales. "I just saw the sun flash off her as she turned...down there, at the other end of the base."

"Have our pilot pick a place to meet her when she comes to rest," Bolan said sharply.

"Okay, now really pull back on the power," said Grimaldi. "Cut it eighty percent, but bring the nose down, too...yep, that's it...a little more."

11:55.

"Hard right. Hard right! More power now. Bring her back level. You got it."

Bolan followed each instruction methodically. Inside he waged a tremendous battle against impending panic.

Gadgets Schwarz pulled out a handkerchief and wiped the sweat from the Executioner's forehead. It was all he could do right now.

Grimaldi's crisp commands streamed through the radio like the sharp attack of a machine gun with the trigger fixed on fire.

"Power way, way back! More! Nose down now. Hold it there and get ready to flare-out when I give the word. Ready, three, two, now! Nose up. Power *off*. Ease the nose down now, ease it down—whoa! Hold it just like that."

"She's in the foam," reported Blancanales.

But Bolan did not look up. He concentrated fiercely. His ears screamed for further instructions. They were not long in coming.

"Right rudder—left aileron.... *Straighten out, baby!* You got it, Sarge."

"No time for any more, Jack. Get down and get the lady out of there."

"That's a roger. I'm tight on her six all the way."

Bolan's chopper was crossing the west end of the runway. It raced to shrink the distance between itself and the still-sliding transport.

Hang on, Anna Charissa. Bolan checked his watch again.

11:57.

Three minutes.

The man in black finished shutting down all the switches, then jumped to his feet and slid open the Huey's port-side door. He stepped out onto the skid.

Numbers falling—numbers falling—numbers falling. It ran like some mad command through his mind.

He was off before the skid touched. He danced to maintain his balance in the slick foam.

He saw Grimaldi's jump-set spew foam in all directions as the fly guy rotated the thrusters for vertical touchdown.

The C-130 was still moving slowly in the foam. It had twisted slightly sideways, was leaning over to touch its port wing tip to the ground. The aerated flood of foam had given it a slick long bed to land in, but there was no buffering feature to it and the touchdown had shredded much of the Herky Bird's underskin. The noise of scraping metal rang in the air like a scream from hell, like one long slip into chaos.

But the scream ended, the crumpling was complete, the fat bird was down and the bruises were nothing, life had been saved.

Bolan slid into a controlled skid that slammed his body into the port side of the big plane. He grabbed a handle, first for balance, then to release the side-door latch.

Before he could open the door, something opened it for him—violently. An unexpected firestorm brought lightning to his eyes and thunder to his ears. It kicked him backward through the air, rudely dropped him hard on his shoulder against the foam-frothed concrete.

His backside slide continued for several more feet, the door and part of the fuselage still pressed between his face and the once-clear sky, a sky now thick with flaming debris and dense black smoke. An acrid stench polluted the air.

Without warning, a second ear-shattering explosion fireballed from the Herky Bird carcass—then a third. Each time, the force rocked the pavement beneath Bolan's body, rattling his head between the concrete and the heavy metal door like a clapper in some grotesque bell.

But it was another bell that tolled there.

It was a silent bell, and it tolled for Anna Charissa.

18

"Oh, my God!" said a horror-stricken April Rose.

The others in the War Room were equally stunned, but said nothing.

Pol's voice on the speakerphone continued.

"The Sarge seems to be okay," he reported, "but he... well, he kinda gives the impression he doesn't want to talk to anybody right now. So we're just laying back out of the way."

"You got a medic to look at him yet?" asked Brognola.

"You know the Sarge. He'll handle it himself. Just a few bumps and scratches. I'd guess a bit of shell shock, too. The door acted as a shield against the brunt of the explosion, but it was one hell of a bang. We were just seconds too late."

"Was anyone else hurt?" asked April. "How about Grimaldi?"

"Jack's fine," Blancanales said. "He got to Striker a few steps ahead of us, but the Sarge was already up and running back into the wreckage. Mack's looking for that lady. I saw him pick up her purse. I found one of her shoes, pretty torn up.

"Every now and then, Grimaldi finds something and takes it over to him, trying to see if the guy's ready to talk yet. But he just looks at it and doesn't say anything, you know. He won't look at anybody. I've never see him like this."

"Any positive ID on the body yet?" Brognola spoke into conference pickup.

"What body? That's just it. So far, all we've got is a shoe and a purse, some red cloth, other fragments. With a bomb that size, we could search all day and not find anything identifiable."

"Let us know what turns up," concluded the Fed.

"Sure thing, Hal." Blancanales rung off.

Leo Turrin cleared his throat. "Hal, the damn press is starting to breathe hard again," he said. "My sources tell me the media boys don't want to sit on this any longer."

"They promised us twenty-four hours," barked Brognola, "and, by God, they're going to keep that promise. I've arranged through the highest channels that they'll get the full story at—what time did we say?"

"Nine," sighed Turrin.

"Yeah, nine o'clock tonight. Anybody prints or broadcasts anything before that is going to have to clean out the toilets of his or her organization for the rest of their career."

"I'll have someone handle the media, Hal," said Turrin. "Forget 'em for now, they'll keep."

April Rose walked over to the console behind Brognola's chair and removed a cassette from the video recorder. She set it aside and replaced it with another.

"Hal," she said. "I was working on something before the crash. I'm not sure yet, but maybe you should take a look."

She pressed some buttons in succession and the machine whirred to life. As the room lights dimmed, she turned to Hal and Leo Turrin.

"This is the first tape that we received from the

terrorists," she explained. "I'm not going to say anything about the second one we got this morning. I just want to see if you notice what I noticed."

Sergeant Larry Shortner's now-familiar image appeared on the screen across the room.

Hal Brognola leaned back wearily.

How many times had he seen this thing now? He yawned quietly in the darkness. He forced himself to stay alert, though it had been a day and a half since he had slept. April Rose, he reminded himself, was no time-waster.

"I don't hear any sound, April," said Turrin.

"Yes, Leo," she agreed. "That's the point."

19

Mack Bolan was at war. In battle after battle, the process of war had made him into a weapon, a thinking, seeing, feeling weapon. He was, perhaps, the ultimate weapon.

The events of his life, and his response to those events—the making of Mack Bolan—had not been unlike the making of a samurai's sword. Like it, he had been repeatedly thrust into the fire, then suddenly withdrawn and hammered flat, then again thrust into the flames and the powerful art repeated over and over again, countless times. His metal had been folded and slammed and pinched into a more and more time-worthy sharpness.

The result was a resilient, tempered weapon with an edge that remained ever-sharp.

And the making of the Executioner was never finished. Each new battle thrust him back into the fire pit.

Whether it was possible to win his war was not important. Fighting it was important enough.

The defeats were in fact many, for they were measured with the blood of innocents.

If the Animals killed only each other, that was fine with Bolan. But when they preyed on the noncombatants, justice required an executioner.

He was not their judge. Their actions had already judged them, and they lived on borrowed time until the sentence could be carried out.

Mack Bolan squinted through the midday sunlight and surveyed the twisted heaps of soot-blackened metal. The jagged piles were spread over a hundred-yard radius. Some of them were still smoking.

He looked at her charred purse still held in his hand and overcame his reluctance to open it. It was—had once been—quite elegant. Where the soot had rubbed off in his hand, the metallic fabric glistened in the noon sun. The cloth lining beneath it had been burned away only in one of the upper corners.

The contents proved ordinary. Some small cosmetic containers, a melted lipstick, keys to a Chevrolet, a slim wallet with the lady's New York State driver's license. There was no cash and no other identification.

Bolan had been witness many times to the destructive power of bombs, in Vietnam especially. He had known men who were whole one moment and bone shards the next.

Something here just didn't sit right.

As powerful as the blasts had been, and as hot as the flames that followed them had been...if the purse and the shoe had survived total immolation, total melt, then some other remnant must surely exist. A part of a tooth, a skeletal splinter, anything.

But of Anna's body, there was nothing.

A large black shadow passed over him. Its outline bore the shape of a long-necked bird.

Just a large jet on final approach, he told himself, not an omen. He let it pass without looking up. He was deep in thought. He needed a decision to move him out of the abyss. He must come to an interim assumption and act on it. Otherwise the darkness would claim him, and immobilize him.

Videotape.... Show business, the realm of false fronts and generated images, the world of illusion and delusion. Bolan coolly reviewed the affair.

If Yareem and his mercenaries had in fact not put their hostage in the Herky Bird, they could use the same hostage over and over again.

A reuseable scam.

This profane altar on which he stood, this smoldering sacrifice. . . . There was no body here, there was no blood.

This black mess was a hoax.

JACK GRIMALDI TRIED NOT TO SLIP on the slick runway.

He stopped short of Bolan by about ten feet, not wanting to intrude too forcefully.

"Sarge, you see what I saw?" Grimaldi was pointing. "Overhead. . . a few minutes ago."

Bolan shook his head tersely.

"That was a Blackbird that just flew over. . . SR-71. Fastest plane there is."

Bolan looked up. His mind was on Nicaragua.

He had formed his decision.

The man-sword was about to be thrust back into the fire.

A Blackbird was about to take on the vultures.

A Blackbird with a Phoenix inside.

20

"WELL, I'LL BE..." began Brognola.

The White House liaison rubbed his chin pensively in the dimly lit War Room. He kept his eyes riveted to the big video image on the opposite wall. "April, by God, I think you've found something here. It's his hands, isn't it?"

"Yeah," agreed Turrin. "Some kind of code, but what's it mean?"

"You tell me," she said.

"It doesn't make sense as Morse code," muttered Brognola.

"I'm glad you confirmed that, Hal," said April appreciatively. "I was beginning to think it was just me."

April stopped the tape machine and waited for the automatic-rewind cycle to end. She removed the cassette and replaced it with the other. She punched the "play" button.

Brognola moved to the image on the screen. He jabbed his index finger at it. "He used his left hand to gesture in the first tape. In this one, it's his right."

"And he seems to be repeating certain hand motions, repeating a pattern," said April. "But check out the taps."

The silent image of Shortner, mouthing words with a bored expression that was probably a mask of fear, revealed a definite pattern to the finger taps of his left hand.

"Yeah, look," said Leo, "he uses the index finger for a single tap, now his middle finger for four more, the next finger once, now back to the index.... What's this telling us? Numbers? Numbers and directions?"

"Longitude and latitude," grunted Brognola. "Want to check it out, April? If we find he's tapping out something like 84.5 with the right hand one way and 14.1 and the right hand's the other way, and he's doing it over and over again on each tape, then we know—" the bulky man moved over to the wall map, rotated a switch to turn up the back illumination "—that he's trying to tell us something about the North Pole or the South Pole.... Or someplace in the Pacific near Peru or in the Indian Ocean, or...." He slapped his palm against Central America. "Or Nicaragua. Pinpointed to the acre."

"I'll get started on it now," said April.

Brognola fired up a cigar from his newly delivered supply.

"I believe our Sergeant Shortner may turn out to be a good guy after all. And that would go for the other vets too," he concluded. "If Yareem had legitimate turncoats, he'd have used one of them on the video instead of Shortner. That's my current guess. Let's see what comes up on those coordinates."

"I know Mack's a one-man infantry division," Leo said, as if thinking aloud, "but.... Well, do you think the president will want to send in the RDF?"

"The president," Brognola said gruffly, "will trust to Striker's reading on that one."

21

IT CAME from the Skunk Works.

Big, black and evil-looking, the SR-71 Blackbird was designed more than two decades ago and had been in active service as a reconnaissance plane since the mid-sixties. But it looked like something out of the far future.

Following the Francis Gary Powers incident, the CIA had expressed a need for something that was "fast as hell" to replace the U-2 spy plane. So they went to the Skunk Works, Lockheed's top secret California factory, and Kelly Johnson, who had designed the U-2. Lockheed and Johnson gave the Agency what it wanted. And then some.

The plane still holds the world records for speed and altitude. Its maximum potentials are still classified; in fact they may not even have been fully tested. Published figures indicate speed to be in excess of Mach 3—almost 2,200 mph—at 85,000 feet plus, with some reports suggesting 100,000 feet.

That's way up there.

Bolan was met by three special ground-crew members.

The three men helped him shed his flight suit and assisted him into the astronaut-type "silver tux," a process that usually takes as long as twenty minutes.

A tall panel truck, its emergency lights flashing, lumbered to a halt. The rear door banged open and out bounced a silver-suited Jack Grimaldi. Trailing behind him were his own wardrobe assistants, all three of them running to catch up with the flier and finish his suit-up procedures.

"It's all set, Sarge," Grimaldi boomed. "Air Force is on the horn now clearing a sky path for this mother." He pointed to the Blackbird's side. "And I hope everyone up there gets the word. They sure as hell ain't goin' to *see* us comin'."

One of the ground crew handed Bolan his helmet. He slipped the cumbersome thing on and the assistant secured its collar fastenings, finally patting the dome and giving Colonel Phoenix the thumbs-up.

Bolan nodded toward the black monster. "You ever flown one of these?" he asked Grimaldi.

Silence greeted his question.

"Yeah," smiled Bolan. "Of course you have. You take the stick. I got some figuring to do."

The two men boarded the SR-71 from a mobile ladder platform. They buckled themselves into tandem seats while the ground crew double-checked their oxygen and communications connections. Grimaldi conferred one last time with one of the Blackbird's regular pilots, then latched the canopy shut.

Pilot-in-command Grimaldi ignited the twin Pratt & Whitney J-58 turbojets and powered up some 32,000 pounds of thrust from each.

He released the brakes and the plane swept out onto the taxiway.

As they taxied to the end of the north-south runway, the fly guy acquainted himself with the array of instruments. "I've flown one of these things exactly once before," he said, with what sounded like a laugh.

Bolan's eyes roamed to the still-smoldering wreck a half-mile distant on the other runway.

He hoped he was right; he prayed they *had* been conned.

The Blackbird swung onto the runway. Grimaldi squared the monster onto the center line and poured on the power. It was fierce.

A mile of runway disappeared in seconds.

The horizon suddenly dropped, then sharply tilted as they banked off toward the Atlantic. Then the horizon itself was gone as the Air Force's fastest flying machine aimed for the blue.

They could enter the supersonic-speed range only over the Atlantic. The Air Force was serious about avoiding sonic booms at the lower altitudes over the States.

Within three minutes Grimaldi brought the plane level at 20,000 feet. "Dipsy-doodle time," he squawked through the intercom. "Hang on."

Bolan was familiar with the term. Dipsy-doodle described a particular technique for slipping through the sound barrier fast and with a minimum of disturbance. The pilot "dipped" the plane down a few thousand feet and brought it level again as the craft crossed into supersonic velocity. After the maneuver, the pilot could turn on the real juice, of which there was a healthy reserve.

Smoothly pressing the throttles forward toward full-out, Grimaldi pointed the Blackbird up again and sighed with satisfaction. The 25,000-foot mark passed before the sigh was complete.

The speed and altitude numbers kept rising fast. Forty thousand feet at Mach 2. Sixty thousand feet at 1800 miles per hour.

Precisely nineteen seconds later, they leveled out at

80,000 feet. The sky above was black, except for the stars shining in from space. Toward the curved horizon, the darkness lightened into a blue veil mixed with the white cloud swirls that slid over the earthier tones on the ground.

The sight was spectacular. And sudden—thus far it had taken longer to suit up for the flight than to actually make it.

Bolan checked one of the dials. The Blackbird was flying literally faster than words could describe: three times the speed of sound.

They had been in the air less than fifteen minutes. The friction of the air rushing over the craft had raised the temperature of its titanium exterior to well over 1000° Fahrenheit. As a result, the plane's body had stretched a full eleven inches longer than when it sat on the ground a mere quarter-hour earlier.

The intercom crackled slightly, then Grimaldi's voice came through. "I'm getting the hang of it. Take a look out there on the right. That's Florida, about a hundred miles east. I don't want to be pushy or nothin', Sarge, but you still haven't told me where to point this dream ship."

"To the scene of the crime, buddy."

"Panama?"

"You got it," said Bolan crisply. "But first we make a little detour. I've just received more interesting new coordinates from April. What say you swing us by the badlands?"

"That's a roger."

Up in front Grimaldi got busy punching buttons on the computerized celestial-inertial guidance system. The navigation did not take long. All the pilot had to do was enter the desired coordinates and the plane would take care of setting the appropriate course. It steered itself.

"All downhill from here, Sarge," noted the pilot. "We just passed the halfway mark for Panama."

It was a miracle plane all right, but the Executioner's mind was running ahead, already roaming the badlands of a place almost a thousand miles to the south-southwest.

And a full fifteen miles below.

LIFE IS TOUGH; only a fool would disagree. But at fifteen miles high the soap opera masquerading as daily life seems no more real than some distant childhood memory. It flashes briefly in and out of awareness.

From this altitude it would take a crowd of men to form more than a speck on the landscape. So how can one man be so audacious as to think he can make any damn difference? It is a rare man to whom it is not so much a question to be answered as a commitment to be realized.

Jack Grimaldi loved this place, the sky, and its timeless space of mind. In this realm, meditation was unavoidable. Here was time enough for a man to sort and shape his values, and room enough to glimpse a grand perspective on his place in the scheme of things.

He thought it might be heaven. The shifting pattern of clouds below changed from one moment to the next, but up here only the constant blue-black of day alternated with the star-speckled black of night. Perhaps God-by-whatever-name wanted all men to see creation from here someday. Perhaps.

For now, however, it was up to a few good men to gather the eternal insights growing in such lofty places, to pluck the promises that ripened here, available to all but perceived by few and truly tasted by fewer.

A good man does what he can. Jack Grimaldi's

clear eyes saw the world as it was. He saw the robbers and rebels feeding on the flocks of the meek and helpless. Something, he knew, *must be done*. Action must be taken. A big task demands a big man. A great task demands a warrior.

Until Destiny confronted him in the person of Bolan, Jack Grimaldi had been fighting an uphill battle against gravity all his life. He raged against it as an enemy.

New he *was* Gravity—"G-Force" as Bolan called him—doing whatever was needed to bring the death-dealers down to earth, down to their knees. One does not argue with Gravity. One respects its existence, as every flier finds out. Otherwise its lesson is repeated again and again until either learning or death happens, whichever comes first. Gravity does not care. It does not care how long it takes, or how many pretty toys or bad boys it breaks in the process. Because ultimately it comes down to this: no gravity—no way to hold together a heavenly body called Earth.

At fifteen miles high, Grimaldi allowed, God's thinking is louder than your own.

If God had intended man to fly, He would gave given him wings.

No, that's bull. God intended man to fly, and therefore He created Jack Grimaldi.

ONLY MINUTES LATER, Mack Bolan relayed new latitude-longitude coordinates to Grimaldi, who fed them into the SR-71's navigation computer. The Blackbird responded by banking very slightly to starboard.

"Life should always be so easy," chuckled Grimaldi.

Bolan concentrated on the huge array of electronic reconnaissance equipment that surrounded him. Brognola had suggested bringing in the RDF. Fine, Bolan had told him, as backups. But this was one score that had reached profound new depths, and he wanted first crack at it himself. His anger now was not steaming, but cool. Cold, in fact, as death itself. He would get a good look at this base camp coming up, and then he would set about ridding the planet of it.

On the dial panel in front of him, important numbers started lining up. The target zone was approaching.

Bolan activated an extremely high resolution video monitor on the console. It was experimental; the plane's camera was sharp enough to pick out the stitches on a baseball from eighty thousand feet. A video enhancement system, like those used on the pictures sent back by the Voyager spacecraft, made the results doubly dramatic.

Despite the Blackbird's half-mile-a-second speed, Bolan instructed the camera to lock onto a tight set of coordinates, and the computer adjusted for parallax and delivered a smooth and undistorted view on the screen.

The monitor showed an area bounded on the west by the Cordillera Isabella, a large mountain range about a hundred fifty miles south of the Honduras-Nicaragua border.

Bolan flipped the scale switch through several levels of magnification as a beeping tone in his helmet signaled that the appointed coordinates had been reached. Something caught his eye near the lower left corner of the screen. He punched in some fine-tuning adjustment. The picture shifted. The object was brought closer to center screen. Again he scaled it up another two levels.

The screen filled with a computerized, jerky but nonetheless extraordinarily clear image of a man lying flat on his back in what appeared to be a small clearing. Scaling up still another level, Bolan noted that the entire right half of the man's face was missing.

Bolan scaled back down and reexamined the surrounding area. To his trained eye, certain shapes and forms now became apparent. There was a small building a few feet from the body. It had been carefully camouflaged.

Further scanning revealed more and even larger buildings, one of which might be a barn of some sort. Then a guard tower. Everything appeared deceptive, problematical, because of the camouflage. But there was no doubt that this was the terrorist base camp.

He scaled down once more to examine the camp in the context of its surroundings. It was backed up against the bottom of a plateau cliff on the north. There were hills and jungle to the south and west. The eastern side was mostly jungle as well, but appeared to be flatter. The airfield would probably be found here, but if so, it was well disguised.

Bolan had only about eighteen seconds of viewing before the picture unraveled and reassembled downrange. But he was satisfied with his probe, probably the swiftest and certainly the softest he had ever made.

"Thank you, Sergeant Shortner," he muttered aloud.

"You found it, huh?" said Grimaldi.

Sure they'd found it.

22

FIVE MINUTES LATER Nicaragua was behind them. The Blackbird passed the coastline near Bluefields and crossed into the Caribbean toward the Canal Zone on a south-southeast heading.

In another ten minutes Bolan would step out of the plane in Panama. In the meantime he studied his mental map of the terrorist base camp and made some calculations. There had been some blank spots in the brief recon, primarily due to the terrorists' skill with camouflage. Now he reasoned out educated guesses to fill in those gaps.

He had seen only one guard tower. There were others, he suspected, possibly three or four, and he approximated their placement. That raised the question of the camp's size. Assuming the airstrip was outside the camp proper, he decided on four or five hundred feet square as a working estimate.

The plateau that rose from the northern end of the camp was computer-calculated as slightly more than two hundred feet high. There would be other guards on top of it to cover that most vulnerable approach route. Those guards would have an extremely advantageous and unobstructed view of all the other approaches. How many men were stationed up there was anybody's guess.

Bolan adjusted the radio frequency. He was channeled quickly through military operators, was finally connected to the base commander at Howard AFB.

Yes, the general confirmed, the OH-6 helicopter he had ordered was ready and waiting for him at the runway turnout reserved for the Blackbird. Orders had been given for the ground crew to start the chopper's engine at the precise moment the SR-71's wheels touched down. And, yes, the Cayuse would be dressed to look like an Army copter. He hoped Bolan would not mind a little wet paint.

"No problem, General," replied Bolan, "and thanks. If you can arrange it, sir, there are a few other items I'll be needing."

He read off a list that had been etched in his mind. The general sounded as though he flinched at one in particular but vowed to comply without further objection.

"I know this puts you between a rock and a hard place, General," Bolan said matter-of-factly, "but I'll need you to have the stuff loaded in that chopper by the time I jump out of this magical mystery ship. And that won't be very long from now."

"From a reading of current classified tactical knowledge, I have come to learn that there are two people for whom we must extend, even break, the laws of physics if required," said the base commander. "And the president of the United States is the other one. You'll have your equipment, Colonel Phoenix, modified exactly as per your specifications."

"There is one final item," said the Executioner. "My pilot needs something to get him onto the *Nimitz*. Preferably something with a tailhook...."

The general paused only a beat. "Will do, Colonel, even if I have to pull it out of thin air."

Bolan thanked him once more and clicked off.

"This is your Captain speaking," said the flyboy in front. "Please extinguish all smoking materials and fasten your seat belts...."

"'Bout time," bantered Bolan. "We've been in this thing almost an hour."

"Fifty-one minutes," corrected the pilot in command. "For my next trick, the anti-G systems in these space tuxedos are essential. I have an idea we're going to take the roller-coaster ride of our lives."

Grimaldi punched a few buttons.

"Hang on to your guts. Here we go—*down*," he said as he fingered the final switch.

The Blackbird rolled over and abruptly fell out of near-orbit. It flung itself toward the ground with an accelerating vengeance.

Grimaldi struggled with his voice. "They say," he managed against the severe gravitational force, "that the human body can withstand as much as forty Gs... for short periods."

"Yeah," groaned Bolan. He let it go at that.

The ground charged up at a thousand feet a second, but that was a mere third or less of the true airspeed. What the ride would have been like if Grimaldi had chosen a purely perpendicular assault was not worth considering.

The acceleration slowed somewhat and equilibrium returned.

Land loomed and the Blackbird made minor course corrections to allow for wind speed and direction. Computerized deceleration made the final moments less intense, and rendered Grimaldi's radio contact with ATC at Howard a safety precaution only. The SR-71 would take care of all the landing procedures, and do them well.

"You know, Sarge," quipped the flier, "even though I sat in this seat and you sat in that one, it sure feels like we were both just passengers on this trip."

"Way it goes, buddy. You'll have plenty to do as soon as we hit the ground and split up."

"I read you, Sarge. The RDF and I will bring in lots of extra choppers. How do you want me to handle air cover for you?"

"I don't want to see or hear any choppers until I've got the lady safely out of the way. I figure you'd be best to bring them through Honduras along the border, then down to the north side of the plateau and wait there for my signal. Once you're inside Nicaragua, make sure you use a well-spaced single-file formation to cut down on the noise."

"Of course," agreed Grimaldi.

"And no lights. It'll be dark then."

Bolan checked his watch and performed fast mental calculations. "No earlier than 1955 hours."

"Wow," said Grimaldi, doing some calculating of his own. "I'm not sure we *could* get there any earlier."

"You'll make it. After you get my signal, it'll take you somewhere between ten and fifteen minutes to come around the plateau to the base camp."

"Okay," confirmed the pilot.

The runway appeared ahead of the Blackbird, perfectly lined up. A moment later the SR-71 touched down.

The black, swept-wing monster fast-rolled down the runway toward the next-to-last turnout. The scale of Howard was appropriate for this freak plane.

In addition to a large ground crew and several assorted vehicles, there was a Navy F-14 Tomcat waiting for Grimaldi and an "Army" OH-6 Cayuse wait-ing for the Executioner. The copter's rotors were already spinning.

The pilot made the turnout and braked to a stop, then shut down the powerful Pratt & Whitneys. The deplaning platform was rolled into place almost by the time he popped the canopy.

The heady stench of burned titanium rushed into Bolan's nasal passages as soon as he pulled off his helmet.

Grimaldi, already standing on the platform, made a waving motion at his own nose and explained that it was normal.

In fact, the SR-71's process of being repeatedly heated up and cooled down caused the titanium body to anneal with every flight, thereby actually making the craft's skin tougher, less brittle. In a sense, then, the Blackbird always landed in better shape than when it had taken off.

"Like a samurai's sword," Bolan said to himself, as he stepped out and stripped down to his blacksuit.

23

THE LITTLE CAYUSE was no Blackbird.

It labored uneventfully across the Caribbean, hugging the waves as the sun grew lower in the western sky. Almost two hundred miles to the west, the deepening shadows of the Costa Rican coastline passed by about fourteen times slower than on the preceding flight.

It was a perfect speed. Bolan had no intention of showing up early in the badlands. His plan called for darkness.

He paralleled the Nicaraguan coast at a safe distance. He was nearing his entry point now, the lower end of the Mosquito coast.

The area took its name from the Mosquito Indians who inhabit that sparsely populated area. Primarily marshland, it is unattractive to most other elements of the population as a place that anyone would want to call home.

The Mosquitos themselves did not much like the Sandinista regime, which had confiscated their farms. Therefore, reasoned Bolan, if the chopper was spotted there, it was not likely to be reported to the authorities.

Bolan crossed the glittering waves, skimmed the marshes, squinted against the huge orange orb of the setting sun.

Within thirty minutes the marshes had thinned out

and were replaced by the rough features of the badlands.

He had timed it accurately. The sun was now half-eaten by the distant mountainous horizon. Dusky shadows stretched out to fill the ground. The sudden coolness gave birth to stiff gusts of evening wind, the uncertain buffeting making his low-altitude approach more treacherous than it already was.

The deepening canyons and rock outcroppings of the badlands demanded keen awareness. Although Grimaldi might laugh and fly such a course blindfolded, Bolan figured he could perform just as well by keeping his eyes open. . . .

He trimmed the blade pitch slightly now, reducing the noisy rotor slap. Where possible he gave wide berth to the echo-prone canyon walls. The buffeting grew more pronounced. The night would be breezy in these parts.

The route he had memorized called for a swing north. Any farther on his present course would bring him directly over the guerilla camp in fifteen minutes' time. The camp would be found, if calculations were correct, at the base of the plateau looming dead ahead in the distance.

The Executioner's plans called for a less obtrusive entry. He steered to the right, away from the camp.

The detour north would bring him around the plateau and also behind a smaller range of rocky hills that paralleled the plateau's eastern side. The roughness of the ground in that area made it the least direct and most difficult approach to the camp. The extra time it would take to get there seemed a wise investment.

It was nearly twenty-five minutes later when he reached the place and several minutes more before he could locate a suitable spot to nest the chopper. He found one, finally, among the tall scrubby brush in a semiclearing of the area where the jungle and desert collided.

Light was scarce as dusk dwindled into darkness. The moon would be full this night, but it would not rise until sometime after midnight. By then the madness would be over, the victor decided.

He tied down the chopper against the on-off gusts of the early night, then quickly moved on to other preparations.

For now, most of the equipment and weapons would be left in the chopper. He must travel light for the soft probe.

Prior to landing, he had spotted a reasonably easy path over and around the first set of hills. Now he double-timed to the crest of the nearest one.

There he pulled out the infrared nightscope and sought a feasible route through the denser terrain toward the camp. A narrow animal trail to the south seemed most promising for the first half of the distance. After that he would make his own path.

The stillness of the night was disturbing.

Only his agility and the occasional gust of breeze existed to cover the sound of Bolan's advance.

And the first sound he heard was not entirely his own.

It was the dull sound of a foot crashing onto his skull.

THE FOOT WAS ATTACHED to a large blond-haired man. The guy had jumped out of a tree and now held a large stick against Bolan's neck in a strangling choke hold. He showed no signs of letting go.

Bolan showed a sign of his own. He twisted, then whipped an elbow into the guy's solar plexus.

Before the pain-filled moan was half uttered, Bolan homed a left to the guy's jaw that sent him flying headfirst into the trunk of the tree from which he had launched his attack.

The big bull was immediately back on his feet and charging. Bolan caught the invader's head in his stomach and pulled the guy over backward with him.

Bolan made a mental note to keep this character's strength in mind. Meanwhile, all of his attention was on the bonecrushing bear hug he found himself wrapped up in. Despite the wearied heaviness of his own arms, Bolan reached up and returned the favor. He then thrust the crown of his own head into the opposing forehead.

For the smallest part of an instant the guy loosened his grip. It was time enough for Bolan to bring up a Fairbairon-Sykes blade to the man's neck. He let it draw enough blood to get the guy's attention.

"It's over," the Executioner announced, catching his breath. "How much more over it gets depends on the next move you're stupid enough to try."

"Wait!" the man wheezed breathlessly in an unmistakably American accent. "You're not one of them. I . . . I thought you were one of them."

A fraction of an inch of sweating skin was all that separated the Executioner's knife from his windpipe.

Bolan kept the blade where it was. "You've got a whole lifetime to tell me who you are and what you're doing here, blondie," he growled.

The American worked at getting the words out. "I know what you're thinking—you think I'm one of them." His voice was a whisper on account of the strain of keeping his neck skin intact. "But that's what they want you to think," he insisted.

Bolan commanded icily: "Keep talking, Bobby."

The Executioner saw the chill run through the guy. There is an old military theory that when the intensity of battle increases, so do the coincidences. In this instance Latchford's voice was unmistakable to Bolan. Latchford's bravura collapsed at the sound of his name.

"Okay, okay. I've only been here since last night. I was on my way the hell out of this hellhole when you—"

"Sure you were. How much did they say they were paying?"

Latchford bristled. "Screw you, turkey. You think I volunteered. Like I told you, man, that's what they want you to think."

"They?"

"The leader's name is Yareem. Etalo Yareem. Dangerous dude. A lot of brains, but they're scrambled. Offered me money, a lot of money. Came right to my damn house. I was on hard times. I let them in. I listened to what they had to say and after I heard it, I told them they could shove it. Then they jumped me. They tied me up like a damn rodeo calf. Next I know, I'm being thrown face first into a dirt hole with a bunch of other guys all telling the same story as me. They helped me get out and here I am. End of story, my friend."

Bolan released his grip on the guy's jugular, but kept the knife starkly in view. He had a gut way of relating to vets, and it was in operation right now.

"Welcome home, Sergeant Latchford." Bolan's voice warmed very slightly.

Bobby rolled back into a sitting position and

rubbed his neck. Looking around, he asked, "Where's the rest of the troops, big guy?"

"Name's Phoenix. Colonel." Bolan sheathed the knife.

The blond guy's blue-green eyes widened. "Yareem's got himself a regular army, you know. I've seen national armies that would be hard put to match his outfit. All due respect, Colonel, but two guys against all that—"

"Let me do the worrying," the nightscorcher said quietly. "Let's get down to specifics."

"Sure thing. But I should tell you that most of what I know is secondhand, from what the other guys told me."

Bolan grunted softly. "Start by drawing me a map. No lights. Draw it here," he commanded softly. Bolan had grabbed the guy's hand and pulled Latchford's index finger into the palm of his left hand. "Start with the perimeters."

The northern boundary, as Bolan already knew, was the bottom of the plateau cliff. There were several buildings in that area, one of them taller than the others, apparently barnlike. Two of the other buildings were barracks buildings, and what remained were various kinds of storage.

The other vets, about eighty of them by Bobby's estimate, were housed in six-foot-deep trenches dug into the compound's southern sector. They were roofed by cut tree branches, leaves and all, laid over a wooden frame. The design served the dual purpose of keeping out both the fierce daytime sun and the curious eyes of anyone who flew over.

Everything, seemingly, was camouflaged—even the guard towers—although some of the cover was removed at night. There were five towers, one at each of the corners and another at the gateway at the mid-point of the eastern side.

Just outside the gate, to the left, were the helicopter pads. This area was separately fenced with barbed wire, as was the main compound. It was camouflaged and so were the choppers, which the Nam guy guessed to number at least three or more. The other vets claimed there were seven or eight.

About a half mile to the southeast of the gate was the airfield. It, too, was camouflaged most of the time. That herculean task fell to the imprisoned vets, forced to work at gunpoint. Covering and uncovering the airstrip was beginning to take its toll on the vets. They were allowed little time to sleep, especially at night, and especially lately, due to what they reported to be a major increase in the number of flights, both day and night. For every flight that landed or took off, no matter how brief the interval, they were required to do camouflage duty.

What Yareem's little air force lacked in modern fighting craft, it made up for in variety. There was a handful of old F-100s, which despite their age sounded pretty good as they flew over, he reported. Also, there was a pair of Lear jets; one of which, curiously, was decked out with camouflage paint. And there was an old C-130 transport with U.S. markings. The helicopters also bore authentic-looking U.S. paint.

"The transport and the painted Lear left around dawn this morning," the guy reported, "and some copters and an F-100 left at first light. Only thing that came back was one of the choppers."

"Any sign of a woman?" Bolan asked.

"Nah, not around here."

"Sure?"

Latchford shook his head, smiled grimly. "If there

was one within fifty miles, I'd be fantasizing it up
right now, you know?''

"What about a Green Beret sergeant. Shortner.
Larry Shortner.''

"Yeah. Sounds familiar. One of the guys mentioned that name to me. Said he was one of the first
guys hauled in, but nobody's seen him since. Rumor
was he stepped out of line and bought it.''

Bolan stood up. "Time to take a closer look. Let's
go.''

"I'd feel more comfortable with a weapon.''

"Wouldn't we all,'' replied the Executioner. He
picked up the nightscoped rifle and handed it to the
former lost American. "I've got a schedule to keep,
soldier. Let's move out.''

It was luck—a mix of preparedness and opportunity—that had brought Bobby Latchford into his
path, into the Phoenix action arena lit by sacred fires
everlasting.

Mack Bolan, the death specialist who had led what
seemed to be a charmed life, knew about *luck*. And
he had his own ideas about the lady.

She came to those who had prepared themselves
the best!

Yeah, the lady would come ride on your shoulder,
and you could feel her rewarding kiss *if* you had
previously taken the time to plan every detail to its
fullest, honed every fighting edge—mind, body and
weapons—to their keenest.

Preparation. Audacity.

Those were the two key ingredients the lady smiled
on favorably in the mystical formula that would
bring the embrace of the charmer known as "Luck.''

And, oh, yeah, there was one more.

A burning anger at the Animals of the world who

lusted to make victims of the innocent and the weak.

So, sure, Mack Bolan had it all—the burning anger, the audacity in battle, the deliberate, careful, detailed preparation in advance, and yeah, most definitely, the honed skills of the pure fighting man.

But Luck was a fickle bitch. She could desert you as fast as she came.

24

THE CAMP WAS IN BLACKNESS.

"They've got infrared binoculars in all the guard towers," the blond guy whispered. "They only turn on lights if they see something move."

Bolan took the rifle back from Latchford, activated the infrared scope and started inspecting the towers. Each contained a pair of guards, one of whom held a submachine gun at the ready while the other scanned the compound and surrounding jungle with what looked to be electronic binoculars.

The man in black watched each of the scanners for two minutes, counting to himself until a definite pattern emerged in the guard routine.

Each guard was handling only a part of a sector, completing a round-trip scan every forty-five seconds, then resting fifteen seconds before repeating the cycle.

Bolan turned the scope toward the top of the cliff.

"I count two, up there," Bolan said softly.

"Damn. Forgot about the cliff," muttered the other man.

The Executioner did not notice any ropes or steps. "They change the guard up there by chopper," he continued in a hushed voice. "Twice a day, I bet noon and midnight."

So there was no minicamp up top. But there were

too many variables all around. In Bolan's estimation the fences of the compound were set dangerously far from the buildings, and there were too many guards with too many night-vision scopes to risk pushing the probe inside the compound's walls. The cliff sentries were particularly bothersome in that regard.

The area housing the vets was separated from the main buildings by an even wider open space, a no-man's-land that bisected the compound from east to west.

Bolan looked again at the barnlike structure. Of all the buildings it was the most likely to contain Anna Charissa or Etalo Yareem, or both. His observation noted an absence of windows in the big building.

There were several doors, however; a couple of large ones on the ground level and at least one on the upper level at the top of a stone stairway. All the buildings, including the barn-size one, had flat roofs.

Bolan returned his gaze to the guards atop the plateau. From that ideal vantage point, nothing could move inside the compound without near-instant detection. Each of the guards' scans took in a wider angle of view than those of the tower guards, therefore their eyes could sweep the entire camp every few seconds. They would have to be removed before any further probe—hard or soft—could have a chance of success.

Bolan checked his watch.

In about ninety minutes the media's soft promise of a twenty-four-hour hold on the most damning aspects of the kidnapping-murder—the "death" of Anna Charissa and the possible involvement of

American mercenaries—would be released to the American public.

Bolan motioned to Bobby for a fall-back along the same track.

Safely out of sight one hundred yards deeper in the jungle that surrounded the camp, the two men stopped briefly.

"What kind of shape are your buddies in?" Bolan asked.

"They're tired, Colonel. Quite a few of them have been here more than two months, and they're wearing thin on hope. They pretty much gave up that anybody knows they're here. Most of them were the same as me—heavy into the loner routine."

Bolan began outlining the forthcoming cleansing by judicial fire. The war was on. "You take the scope rifle and dig yourself in back where we did the recon. You'll have to sit tight for twenty minutes or so. Keep your eyes on the sky for my signal."

"Don't underestimate Yareem's men, Colonel. They can bring down a chopper with a single shot."

"Not a chopper—too noisy," said the man in black.

"If you're thinking of climbing the cliff, it's more than twenty minutes...."

The tall guy looked up at the sky. "I plan to grow wings. Okay, hear me. You'll have to count off the time...five minutes from my signal—two tiny red flashes—then you get to the vets and start knocking off guards."

"Gotcha, Colonel."

"This could be a suicide mission, buddy," the Executioner said. "Now's your chance to change your mind."

"Five minutes from your signal," confirmed the blond guy.

Bolan smiled grimly, turned and was gone.

LATCHFORD LOST SIGHT AND SOUND of him in seconds. Then, the blond guy also left that place and slowly stepped back to the front, his heart and mind racing to beat each other.

This Colonel Phoenix, he thought, had projected an air of certainty. Overwhelmingly so. He made the impossible seem an accomplished fact.

But it wasn't a false-front bravado with this guy. It was some quiet, resolute certainty in himself that did not depend on circumstances for validation. And yet at no time did the guy seem blind to the realities of the circumstances.

Wholeness cannot be described by any one of its parts. The guy was whole, all right: somehow just a little larger than life.

But the guy was *human*.

Hell, decided Bobby Latchford, human enough to be a friend. Damn, the guy did seem familiar. Those eyes, especially. Icy, ancient. Glacier eyes. Something about that face, too. But Bobby could not place it.

He rebuked himself for what the booze and drugs had done to his memory.

If he hadn't been half in the bag on a binge yesterday afternoon, he might have given Yareem's stooges more than that single wild swing that ended up missing the target and smashing the framed photograph of his parents on the wall.

Latchford spat onto the damp jungle floor. He would draw on everything now—his background in the jungles of Nam, in the roughest precinct in Phila-

delphia, in being one of life's goddamn survivors—
all of it.

And he would survive the next thirty minutes. He
would not let himself down.

He'd stake his life on that.

He had a feeling that the tall guy with ice for eyes
was staking his life on it too.

25

THE STARS WERE BRIGHTER NOW, as bright as they would be at anytime before the post-midnight moon-rise.

Little of that illumination, however, reached the jungle floor, as Bolan cut his way catlike through the twisted tangle.

The jungle parted at the small rocky bluff, skirting it to either side. Some distance beyond the hill the jungle would reconsider the trial separation and rejoin itself. Just short of that reconciliation was the spot where Bolan had tied down the chopper against the uncertain gusts of the night.

He climbed easily to the top of the little hill and, peering over its crest to the west, froze stock-still. Whispered voices wafted across from the far side, almost indistinguishable in the furtive wind.

Starlight slowly revealed the owner of one of the voices and, a moment later, another. The two were spaced several feet apart, little more than a matched set of shuffling shadows.

The silenced Beretta slid noiselessly from its leather nesting place and snuggled into the Executioner's right palm.

He watched the terrorists' cautious advance, waiting for the pair to get within forty feet.

While one of the men was preoccupied with idle chatter, looking into the darkness, he failed to notice a dark red hole appear in his partner's forehead. Nor did he see the second hole that opened up in his partner's throat.

All he saw—his last sight on earth—was a series of pencil-point firejets that were now flashing him his own farewell.

The Beretta had spoken its death sentence.

The Executioner dragged the bodies under cover of a thorny bush. Tomorrow, the vultures would find them.

A khaki field cap belonging to one of the dead men was lying in the path. Bolan picked it up, intending to toss it onto the bleeding heap, then changed his mind and instead stuck it on top of a thorny bush a few feet from the bodies.

With the terror troopers eliminated from underfoot, the way was clear for Bolan's advance on the Cayuse parked beyond the short plateau.

When he reached it, he opened the rear door and began unloading the special equipment ordered from the base commander at Howard earlier that afternoon. One of the items was a small black box. He opened it, removed an even smaller black box that he slipped into one of his sleeve pockets. Then he tossed the original box into one of the chopper's small storage compartments.

He slung the Uzi, then hefted a very large and long black bundle to his shoulder. He relatched the door and started back up the rock hill.

He set the package down in a clear area short of the top, a spot moderately protected from the wind. Carefully he unrolled the black fabric, revealing some dark-colored aluminum poles, another nightscope and an automatic pistol. All of the ordnance had been deliberately arranged within the folds of the fabric to minimize any noise during this phase.

Deft hands worked immediately, transforming the fabric and poles into a man-size kite. In a matter of minutes a black hang glider stood assembled in the windless space. Memories of Carl Lyons's recent exploits with a similar sky toy in Catalina warmed his heart even as it sent a chill of anticipation up his spine.

Bolan stood and attached to the Uzi a special break-away elastic that would keep it pressed to his chest until called for.

Detaching the kite from a temporary assembly mooring, Bolan lifted the winged apparatus and strapped himself into its harness, testing each belt as he used it.

A quick inspection showed everything in shape. He had ordered the kite rigged with silenced Oberdorfer 9mm automatic pistol, locked in register with the infrared nightscope. The entire gun assembly pivoted smoothly in a ball-and-joint mount on the main right strut.

He waited for a momentary gust to give out, then turned himself and the kite around to face the area near the chopper. The nightscope made easy work of locating the dead man's hat where he had left it stuck to the bush. He squeezed the trigger a single time and saw the dark hole appear in the cap's brim simultaneously with the automatic's muffled sneeze.

Not satisfied, he made a slight adjustment to the scope, then repeated the test. This time a hole appeared precisely at the junction of the brim and the body of the cap.

He ejected the Oberdorfer's clip, added two 9mm bullets to replace the test shots, reinserted it. Practice was over. Time for the real thing.

As Mack Bolan had learned a lifetime ago, in a Mafia war experience in Hawaii, the Rogallo-winged little hang-gliding crafts could be valuable tools in certain situations, unpredictable hazards in others.

The breeze was up again. These were not ideal hang gliding conditions.

Bolan waited for the mental flow of negative considerations to conclude. Then he kept the kite's nose low and into the wind and stepped the remaining few feet to the crest of the hill.

He fought the gusts to keep himself on the ground.

Sensitive ears picked up the shushing sound of an approaching steady breeze as it raked over the leaves of the nearby jungle.

The breeze kept its promise. The Executioner ran into the sky and was airborne, bound for the vultures' nest, bound for the vultures.

HE DIPPED THE NOSE AGAIN to pick up speed, then swooped up and banked left, first heading east away from the terrorist camp to gain altitude in lazy spirals.

When the glider reached twice the height of the plateau, he shifted his weight again, and the killer kite glided toward the next objective.

Floating high above the cliff, he scanned its edge with the high-power infrared scope and made sure of the count: two sentries, several hundred feet apart. One maintained a position above the center of the compound. The other, near the eastern edge, eagle-eyed the airstrip and helicopter areas.

The second would be first. Since the lookout man was standing his ground only feet from the edge, care would have to be taken to ensure the guy's body did not fall into the camp's chopper pad area. That would ruin the surprise part of the party the Executioner was planning for Yareem.

The night breeze cooperated, staying light but steady.

Bolan made his swooping move. He dipped the glider's leading edge and let the control bar ease back momentarily until he found an altitude a few feet above the plateau. He was coming in behind and to the left of the unwary sentry. As he neared the plateau's edge, he angled a sharp right and immediately sighted in on the guy's left ear.

A flutter of the night-kite Dacron sails caught the man's attention. His alertness was rewarded with a 9mm parabellum entering his eye, followed immediately by a second slug that ripped through his teeth. The body collapsed in a short slide that left a leaking head peering over the cliff in a sightless stare.

Meanwhile, the man in bat black fought the craft back to straight-and-level in the stiff windward draft that rushed up over the cliff's edge. He faced the kite into it, raised the nose and let it take him in a drift some fifteen yards to the north. Then he dipped the nose back down and found appropriate position for a death approach to the remaining guard.

But as the nighthawk closed in, he saw no sight of the guy. No trace in the nightscope. Quickly, he pushed out on the control bar to gain a few feet.

The higher perspective revealed the answer. The sentry had moved to a more comfortable position, was flattened on the ground and prone between a pair of large boulders. He was scanning the camp's far boundaries.

Bolan swung the glider to the left and dived the rig out over the edge of the cliff.

There he fought the stiffer currents for his ride. He

sailed just beneath the cliff top, daringly close to the wall itself and only a few hairs below the solitary sentry's still elevated line of sight.

At the memorized location, he yanked the kite up with the current and came floating feet-first into the binoculared eyes of a very shocked terrorist.

The sentry stopped in mid-grope for his own weapon and admitted a pair of 9mm visitors into his head, at the throat and the temple. The visitors stayed only long enough to put out the lights and then they exited in massive back doors of their own making.

The Executioner left that place in a sweep, his high arc soaring him back to where Bobby Latchford awaited a signal.

26

BOBBY LATCHFORD was not looking up.

He was looking at three khaki-clad soldiers slowly patrolling the dusty perimeter that ran along the outside of the camouflaged barbed-wire fence. Although they were about a hundred feet away, they were moving in his direction.

Latchford silently lifted the rifle and brought the powerful nightscope to his right eye. The image that filled the viewfinder made him shudder.

It was apparently not a routine patrol. The threesome carried AK-47s in ready-for-business fashion. Their movements were the actions of men who expected, very soon, to find what they were looking for.

What they were looking for was one Bobby Latchford.

One of the three terror guards left the path to examine the nearby jungle underbrush. A moment later he rejoined the others, his curiosity apparently satisfied.

Latchford watched with growing horror as the pattern was repeated approximately every dozen feet. When the trio approached to less than forty feet from him, Bobby Latchford found himself frantically preoccupied with his chances of being discovered on one of the off-track forays.

The man's pounding heart was a jungle drum beating out urgent run-like-hell messages to his paralyzed feet.

The blond guy was not a cowardly man, by any means. He had distinguished himself as a tough soldier in Vietnam. He had distinguished himself as a tough cop in a tough city.

But all that was long ago and this situation was different. Lack of preparation, he guessed, both mental and physical. His fighting days were over, or so he had thought. Wasn't that why he quit the force in Philadelphia?

Too many dead bodies had littered his mind and weighted his aging shoulders. Like when he bush-whacked that Phoenix guy, he thought. Bobby wouldn't have killed him. He had planned only to subdue him, take his weapons, buy himself half a chance of walking out of this nightmare.

Where the hell is Phoenix!

He tried squeezing himself deeper into the brush cover around and behind him. He had reached the limit of this particular hole. But he could pull the scope rifle in a bit closer, and when he did so he felt its cool barrel touch the damp, chill skin of his chest. His entire body was soaked in sweat. He rubbed his right palm against his pant leg, then returned his finger to the trigger. He wondered if it was the last move he'd ever make.

The sounds of shuffling footfalls scraped closer. His mind was exploding with ugly memories and gruesome pictures from the past. He was on the verge of screaming.

NAM! Shit! It's Nam again! I'm gonna die! I'm gonna die! I'm gonna—

All sound ceased in his ears. Through the slits of his squinting eyes, he saw only feet.

Count 'em! commanded his whirring brain.

...three...four—*two missing!*

Scorching stress pains streaked through his chest and back. He was sure he had not breathed in three or four minutes, improbable as that was.

Where the hell are those other two legs?

The answer rustled a bush not four feet away, nearly stopping his heart. Every muscle in his right arm began to spasm. In a moment, surely, they would hear him.

One of the men on the path dropped his weapon and collapsed beside it.

An instant later, the second man keeled over, face first, into the dirt....

The third man heard the bodies crumple and left the brush just long enough to catch a parabellum himself. It came crashing through the crown of his head with such force that the impact pitched his body backward into the place from which it had just emerged.

There followed a silence like Bobby Latchford had never known, even in that crazy Asian war: strange, thick...*crisp.*

Again he thought—truly believed—he would scream.

THE TENSE, FRIGHTENED FACE of the blond man finally appeared in the scope.

Bolan dared not bring the glider below sixty feet. Even at that height he incurred risk of detection by the tower guards at the opposite side of the compound. Fortunately, the camouflaged roofs of the towers restricted their aerial vision to a degree. And would they be looking for a silent substance in the sky?

Latchford did not look up, still bathed in shock. The deaths he had witnessed would have to suffice as a signal to get inside the compound and start his five-minute count.

Near the north end of the compound, a sliver of light briefly appeared and disappeared near the two-story barn building. Bolan had to maneuver back across his track to be sure he had really seen it. The infrared scope showed the light coming from a crack in a large doorframe on the ground floor. No other signs of life were apparent as he guided the craft over the structure.

The flat, camouflage-painted roof of the building would suffice as a landing field. Circling it once, he saw no signs of guards. He lined things up.

His steep approach caused the wind ribbon on the glider's nose strut to flutter wildly, making a sound like the bats that haunt hell to avenge horror. Bolan flared out sharply as he passed the roof's edge, bent his knees slightly to absorb the landing shock, and set down easily and quietly. He dipped the nose into the wind and unsnapped himself from the harness.

He fished out three screw-hooks from a pocket and twisted them into the roof surface. He lashed three elastic "shock cords" from the glider to the roof, lest it drift off the edge and prematurely announce his presence.

Crouching, Beretta in hand, Bolan quickly slipped over to the western edge of the roof. Below it, according to his aerial observations, there was a second-floor door at the top of a cement stairway.

He lowered himself to the landing.

The door was unlocked and apparently unguarded.

He opened it a crack. He saw the guard about ten feet inside the door, silhouetted in a brilliant wash of light that emanated from the barn's ground level. The guard, his back turned and oblivious to his duties, was enraptured by the activities taking place under the lights.

Two seconds later the guard became oblivious to everything else in life.

The Executioner's garrote tightened around his neck. The blacksuited justice-maker dragged the still-twitching corpse back into the deep shadows near the doorway.

Then he stepped toward the edge of the balcony and took a good look at the spectacle that had held the former guard so spellbound.

Once his eyes had become accustomed to the bright glare of the barn's interior, a familiar face loomed out of a stage center under the lights: Sergeant Larry Shortner, "star"—not of stage and screen, but of recent terrorist video productions.

Shortner was sitting behind a simple wooden table in full uniform, including beret. Bolan could not hear what the soldier mumbled, but he must have said it wrong because a camou-uniformed guy was screaming at him in a thick accent.

"You are supposed to point at the camera when you say that, you *imbecile!*" screeched the voice. "We must begin again. Pronto! Pronto!"

The former Green Beret sergeant lowered his head, seeming to look for strength. A guard stepped up behind him and forced Shortner's head back into position. Shortner shook his head free of the guard's hands, said nothing.

The man who had been shouting turned and stalked out of the lights and back past the cameras. Cables and wires were snaked sloppily everywhere. At least once the little man had to catch himself from tripping. He stopped behind a pair of men seated at a larger table stacked full of TV monitors and related audio and video equipment.

"Pronto! Pronto!" he repeated impatiently.

Bolan guessed this noisome creep to be Etalo Yareem, leader of the hi-tech terrorists, the man he most wanted to see. And see dead.

Bright as the studio lights were, they were concentrated on only a small portion of the large room. The contrast made it difficult to see into the deep gray shadows that filled the rest.

The four-foot-wide balcony that was the second floor ran along three sides of the interior. There was no walkway above the "stage" of the makeshift studio, at the opposite wall from where Bolan stood. To the right of the stage area were the closed double doors he had seen from the air minutes earlier.

Iron-barred jail cells were spaced along the walkways to either side. All were dark. None showed signs of movement.

Below, on the ground floor, the videotaping session had resumed. This time, the American sergeant obediently raised his arm to point at the camera, but again a voice screamed at him. But this time it was a very different voice.

This time it was a woman's voice.

"Don't do it, soldier! This is Anna. I tell you not to cooperate with them!"

It was the firm, insistent voice of Anna Charissa.

Bolan could see the faint outlines of her face and hands pressing through the bars of the cell from where the voice had come.

"Gag her!" shouted the terror leader, ripping off his earphones and slamming them on the table. He said it again in Spanish, plus some other choice words.

Two guards rushed up concrete stairs and entered the woman's cell. One of them held a battery-powered lantern in his left hand as he aimed his AK-47 at her head with the right.

For Bolan the new light provided his first good look at the lady he had traveled in the last twenty-four-hours-plus through almost five thousand miles of hell to find.

Her body was lean and youthful, at least what was not covered by a too-large man's khaki shirt worn unbuttoned over a white half-slip and bra. Her dark hair fell in tangles to her shoulders. Bruises marked her legs and face.

And the face was strong and beautiful and highly indignant. Her eyes sparkled with energy.

One of the soldiers shoved her to the floor, then knelt over her and fastened a gag. He yanked it tight behind her head.

Anna Charissa ignored the rifle pointed at her by the other soldier, kept kicking and scratching and biting until each offending part of her anatomy had been tightly bound by her abusers. Even when she could not curse them aloud, she cursed them with her eyes.

Both men, now bruised themselves, laughed at her. Then they left the cell, and one of them carefully relocked its door. The other one walked back down the stairs and took up his former position.

The first guard remained, at first impatiently walking back and forth several times, then seating himself at the edge of the walkway, letting his feet dangle over the edge. He unstrapped his rifle, placed it in his lap, leaned back on his elbows.

The Executioner stepped out of the shadows and approached the guard. He started to pull out the garrote again, then changed his mind and palmed the knife instead.

Bolan was committed now to an inflexible sequence of events which, once set into motion, must be followed through to completion. Not a move nor moment could be wasted.

He came up behind the guard, immediately covered the man's mouth with his left hand and pulled him backward onto the knife. The blade thrust up squarely into the kidney. It was a traumatic injury that killed the guy almost instantaneously. The Executioner left the knife in its bloody home and whipped his right arm out and around to grab for the fast falling AK-47. He plucked it muzzle-first from midair as it slid off the man's lap toward the ground ten feet below.

In another smooth single motion he retrieved the knife, wiped it and replaced it in its sheath, then laid the rifle across the dead man's chest and eased the guy's head to the concrete.

He found the cell keys in the man's pocket and quietly removed them. Stepping back to the cell door, he glanced around only once to see if anyone had seen him yet.

Someone had.

Both men's eyes locked in register across the noisy, distracted barn studio like eternity frozen in the quick heart of the hellground.

It was Larry Shortner's gaze that broke away first.

Suddenly the former sergeant stood, picked up the table in front of him and launched it angrily at the camera. Camera and cameraman crashed back to the ground in a clatter of lumber and metal and bone.

A gaggle of guards descended on Shortner, but heroically he shoved them off. Another soldier knocked him in the back of the head with a rifle butt, leaving the burly ex-marine dazed but still standing.

"Imbeciles!" shouted Yareem to his men. "No, do not shoot him!" The terrorist leader drew his own side arm and briskly marched over to the misbehaving sergeant, now held in place by four men.

Yareem stared into the man's eyes. "American asshole," he hissed through clenched teeth.

Shortner spit into Yareem's face.

Yareem brought his knee up hard into Larry Shortner's crotch. The sergeant doubled up, bellowed in pain.

"Tie him to the chair," barked Yareem. "He will cooperate now. Later we will reward him for his tantrum."

Yareem's men began reassembling the little studio. A second camera was hauled out of the shadows and mounted in front of a new table.

God bless Larry Shortner, said Bolan to himself, in all sincerity. During the commotion, Bolan had opened the cell and untied a startled Anna Charissa. They both made it all the way to within a foot of the door. . . .

Before they were noticed.

27

THE GUARD WHO WALKED IN through the second-floor outer door at that moment was, given the casual manner in which he entered, not expecting to see anything unusual.

The guard certainly did not expect to see a tall black apparition who had eyes that held the power of life and death. The man no doubt thought he had glimpsed death personified. He had.

While the intruder fumbled his automatic rifle into position, the Model 93-R whispered a death note and signed it with a red dot above his left ear. The dead man's finger squeezed the automatic's trigger in postmortem seizure. A wild but harmless spray alerted the barn studio to the Executioner's presence.

Suddenly Larry Shortner was no longer the center of attention.

"The woman!" shouted Yareem.

Bolan pushed Anna to the ground just as a thundering storm of slugs perforated the walls and doorframe. They kept moving, she in front of him, crawling over the dead guard in the doorway and out to the steps. There Bolan lifted her until she could grasp the edge of the roof, then pushed her feet until she could manage the rest.

Inside, guards rushed along the inner landing. Bolan leaned back into the doorway, pulled the Uzi away from his chest into firing position and let it rip through them.

The messy pile-up of dead and dying would stall the others only a few moments. Bolan slammed the door shut. He hoisted himself to the roof with all the strength he had.

As soon as he was up, guards burst through the doorway, firing indiscriminately into the surrounding darkness. Seeing nothing, they charged down the stairway and fanned out in all directions from the barn building.

Above them, on the roof, Bolan crouched and moved quickly to the hang glider, grabbing Anna's elbow en route. Reaching the hang glider, he cut loose the shock cords holding down the craft.

The Chinese had used man-carrying kites for warfare more than 700 years ago, though Bolan doubted they took passengers along. Now he calculated that Anna Charissa was light enough as far as the kite itself was concerned. The rest would depend on the wind.

Bolan motioned for her to come around behind him. She put her arms around his waist. Working quickly, he secured her to his back with the extended harness.

The wind ribbon was limp. He wet his index finger and checked the wind.

There wasn't any.

He calculated the consequences of jumping off the roof in a zero wind condition. At best they would not die in the crash.

Wind or no wind, it was time to try the sky.

He faced the kite toward the helicopter-pad area. If they could get any kind of glide at all, their best chances were in that direction.

He whispered sharply to Anna, "Pick up your feet."

Pushing forward into a run, they gained speed but little lift in the ten yards before the roof ran out. Then they were off, but not exactly airborne.

The glider plunged at a steep angle. Less than six feet from the ground, Bolan felt the reassuring tug that told him they were flying now, not falling. Then they gained some altitude, if fifteen feet could be considered much of an altitude. They would need a lot more than that to disappear into the night.

Suddenly the night itself disappeared as searching spotlights and other lights came ablaze within the compound.

A pair of soldiers were running around the corner of a building. One of them looked up and began firing at the giant black lepidoptera.

Bullets whizzed by Bolan's head, tore through the Dacron fabric, gave the big moth a large number of instant moth holes.

The Uzi sprang away from his chest to respond in kind, delivering death doses to the ground-bound duo.

In the new light Bolan could see the veterans charging their guards, trying to get across a no-man's-land between themselves and the main buildings created by machine-gun fire.

Some apparently had real weapons, but most did not, happy to have anything, a hunk of lumber or a length of barbed wire or just plain bare hands, to unleash their fury at the enemy. Those with weapons had undoubtedly captured them from dead guards. And Bobby Latchford, he hoped, had thought to strip the three dead soldiers outside the fence.

The glider was becoming less and less airworthy by the moment.

More slugs ripped through the cloth sails and lift was virtually lost. The bullets had come from a chopper pass. A glance toward the pads showed more of the copters starting up. Sharing the air with helicopters would reverse any advantages the glider might have demonstrated thus far. It was time to land.

Bolan risked a right bank and headed for the chopper pads. The black craft came down hard, just clearing the barbed wire, practically disintegrating on impact.

"I'm fine," Anna said matter-of-factly before he could ask. It was the first time she had spoken to the big guy—except for the quick conversation that had flashed between their eyes when he first pulled her to freedom.

This is one tough lady, thought Bolan, impressed.

He cut the both of them out of the harness, and together they crawled out of the tangle of bent aluminum tubes and tattered synthetic cloth.

The terrorist soldiers pursuing them on foot had been stopped by the barbed wire. While some tried climbing through, others continued firing automatic rifles into the darkness.

Bolan pushed Anna behind him and sprayed several tight figure eights with the Uzi into the crush at the fence, immediately taking half of the soldiers out of the game. He spent no time watching the bodies roll but grabbed the woman's arm and moved on toward the pads.

As far as he could tell, they had not yet been seen by the men in the two choppers that were still revving up on the ground. He cautioned Anna to lie flat on the ground, then ducked around the far side of the nearest helicopter and yanked open the pilot's door. The AutoMag came into play. Two men became separated from their brains, wasted gray matter spewing out of holes that would never heal.

The Executioner roughly pulled out the pilot's body and waved Anna to the back. He opened the rear door and boosted her in. "Lie perfectly flat," he commanded, then latched the door and jumped into the pilot's seat.

The helicopter was an Argentina-manufactured version of the Hughes OH-6 Cayuse, which meant all the instruments were labeled in Spanish. Basically, however, a chopper is a chopper. It was already running, and it was armed with an XM-27 machine gun remote-operated by the pilot. It would do.

Bolan goosed the throttle, changed the blade pitch and lifted out of there. As soon as they were up, he leaned over and opened the opposite door, then banked steeply right and shoved out the remaining dead body. Now he reversed the craft into a left bank and secured the door, before leveling out. He figured the 170-pound weight loss would lighten the load factor and considerably improve the flying characteristics of the little Cayuse.

THE DEAD COPILOT CRASHED to earth a few feet from the pad area, almost directly in the path of Etalo Yareem himself.

The terrorist leader was aghast. He ran over to one of the waiting copters and barked at the pilot to get out. When the man did not move fast enough, Yareem reached in and yanked him to the ground, muttering, "Imbeciles! All of them!"

The *comandante* climbed into the seat and

slammed the door, ordering the copilot to take off. "Pronto! Pronto!" he yelled, pointing to the fast-disappearing helicopter that contained the lady and the son of a bitch in black.

Yareem fumed. Who did this intruder think he was dealing with? What made him think he could take what belonged to Etalo Yareem?

WITH ANNA CHARISSA out of Yareem's hands, it was time to unleash Grimaldi, who was, Bolan prayed, a mere ten minutes away with the strike-and-rescue copter cavalry. He fished out the tiny radio and gave the go-ahead.

Whether or not Grimaldi replied, Bolan did not know. Any transmission was drowned out by the cacophony of raging lead projectiles ripping in through the left-side window of the Cayuse and exiting uselessly out the right door.

Bolan whipped the stick down and left, diving the little copter below another onrushing chopper, the one that had earlier riddled the glider and was at this moment issuing near-deadly shots at the Cayuse. Now it sped past, spun up into a high-banked one-eighty, then straightened out for another pass.

In the meantime Yareem's chopper showed up. It invited itself into the dogfight as a third player. Coming off a sharp arcing turn and into a dead-on run toward Bolan from the opposite direction, Yareem's machine gun was already set to blazing.

The Executioner ignored the first copter for the moment and spun his ship about to face Yareem's. He sent a tracer line of luminous death flying into the *comandante*'s cockpit. The stream missed Yareem but ripped through the copilot's throat, leaving the guy's head momentarily in midair before it bounced back off the headrest and tumbled into his dead lap.

Yareem stopped firing and made a panicky grab for the controls as his chopper pirouetted helplessly in midair.

Sitting duck that Etalo Yareem now was, there was no time to finish him off. Bolan radically altered the tail-rotor pitch and whipped his craft around to take on the other already charging chopper.

But the guy was closer than Bolan had figured. He cut short the intended one-eighty, swiped the Uzi off his chest with his right hand and sent its rapid-fire lead thundering out the left window, shattering what was left of the Plexiglas and doing likewise to the pilot-side window of the opposing craft. Then likewise again to its pilot.

Still hovering in the middle of two out-of-control choppers, and with the airspace available to him fast shrinking, Mack Bolan caught the unmistakable odor of death's approach.

Time slowed. The sequence of events that now took place in less than a half-second might have appeared to an observer as simultaneous, but in the superreality of death-so-near there was a definite chronology.

His every sense sharpened.

The staccato rotor-slap of three different pitches from three separate helicopters warped into a hollow bass tone, a backbeat to death.

The warrior's peripheral vision widened impossibly and grew superacute, bringing into telescopic focus the shock-frozen eyes of Yareem on his right. The little *comandante*'s nostrils flared widely above a mouth grotesquely open in a silent scream at the approaching doom. The image seemed no farther away than twice the length of the Executioner's arm.

At the real end of the Executioner's arm, however, trained fingers obediently twisted the main rotor pitch to zero and flattened the throttle to nothing, turning the normally agile little craft into a plummeting rock.

In the subjective sense of time, the fall from space was slow, precise, exact. In actual fact, it was wild enough to drop Bolan and his passenger right out of the field of action. They were no longer participants. They were witnesses of a hell sport that would split the night sky.

Bolan and Anna watched as the two remaining helicopters fenced rotor-to-rotor like two gladiators.

A severed rotor tip from the fray flicked away and glanced off the plastic windshield bubble of the Executioner's fast-falling, slow-falling craft.

Then the rotor housing of one of the clashers gave way with a tortured metal-on-metal groan. The losing copter fell into the side of the other and burst brilliantly into sparks and flames.

The thus-entangled wrecks spiraled in an almost lovely swan dive of death. They disengaged about halfway to the ground, one of them disintegrating in a blinding ball of fire.

The resounding explosion slammed time back into place, and that place was here and now.

The jolt rocked the Executioner's mind even as the blast's actual shock waves rocked his wingless flying machine, itself more than halfway bent on digging its own grave.

Bolan whisked the throttle back to full and again switched the pitch, shuddering the chopper to the brink of a death rattle as every nut and bolt strained to maintain. Just maintain.

Inertia argued hotly that "up" was a lost cause.

The little copter's skids hit flat bottom and bounced the machine awkwardly skyward again.

The force of the impact stretched the flexible rotors to within a millimeter of break point, and narrowly missed grazing the tail strut. A hair's more stress and the turboshaft itself would have bent, resulting in the helicopter tearing itself apart in a fraction of a second.

So, yeah, it was that close.

The blades bit solidly into the air now. Most traces of wobble subsided as Bolan steered around the bright column of flames that had been one of the losing combatants.

Only the sharpest eyes on the war-torn ground could have distinguished his helicopter from either of the others. For all Bolan knew, the guards were assuming that he was Yareem, and that suited Bolan just fine. . . so long as none of the American vets got the same idea and began taking aim. It was a real possibility.

It had been a lifetime ago—but less than a minute by his chronograph—since he'd radioed Grimaldi. If each of the next nine minutes were as long as that last one had been, then those brave vets were never going to make it.

The Executioner tried the little radio again.

There was no response.

28

"ANNA!"

Bolan had to shout to be heard above the rotor roar. "You all right?"

A calm, delicate hand came to rest on his right shoulder. "I don't know who you are, fighting man, but I am grateful. And don't worry about me—I'm still very much in one piece."

He turned and met her smile, returned it. She wore a white flight helmet she had found in the passenger area. Bolan lifted his right hand from the main stick and lightly rapped the helmet with his knuckle, giving her a wide smile at the same time. "Smart lady," he chuckled. "Stay smart and get back down, hear?"

She pouted, obeyed.

The safe thing to do was to get the lady free of the fire zone. But Bolan saw only too clearly that the safe thing was at cross-purposes with some other important things.

Like making the odds a little better for those vets scattered all over the south end of the compound, most of them using the darkness in ways learned from the Vietcong, and whenever possible using sticks and stones against real weapons.

Bolan decided on a route that would take him directly over the guard tower nearest the main gate, where a machine gun was cutting off the vets from the main buildings.

Bolan did not—*could not*—overlook the fact that the vets had denied themselves the relatively safe escape route into the jungle to the south. They had chosen instead to stay and fight, despite the odds. There was no deserting them now. Not for Mack Bolan.

There was, therefore, no question. And ultimately, no cross-purposes. All purposes would be served, God willing.

Bolan lurched the chopper toward the offending tower, found his targets therein and opened the doors of hell for two fast-dying machine gunners. He ripped them in two with a stream of 7.62mm door knockers from the copter's XM-27.

Bolan's target status was immediately returned, the incident having identified which side was commanding the copter. He attracted fire from several quarters at once, like tacks to a magnet. But the chopper was already passing out of the compound area, and the projectiles produced no serious damage.

Something, however, had caught Bolan's eye as he flew over the dead men's tower.

He pulled several Gs in a tight banking reversal and came back around to take another look.

He looked, and he saw, and he knew he had seen right the first time.

A blond guy was about to get himself scalped by a pair of terrorist troopers. One of them stood behind Bobby Latchford, holding his arms while the other made ready to slice the guy into lunch meat with a machete.

Flying a helicopter close to the ground normally required two hands and both feet, not to mention an acute sense of balance. Rotorcraft are highly sensitive machines and many otherwise excellent pilots just never get the hang of it.

Mack Bolan did have the hang of it, to a degree that had to be called mastery. He had taught himself, from close observation of pilot activities when aboard the whirlybirds of Nam, to crash landing one of the damn things in the new battleground of Libya—with many occasions, both recreational and fraught, in between.

The Executioner swooped the Cayuse down and tore along a low track, skimming the ground.

He poked the life out of the knife wielder with the XM-27. He put the chopper into an abrupt hover, leaned out the smashed side window, drew the Auto-Mag from its belt holster with his left hand and blew the head clean off the guy holding Latchford.

As the headless hulk keeled over, Bobby went with him, still in the dead man's grip.

For a moment Latchford was evidently unsure whether he was alive. Then he bounced up and ran toward the low-hovering chopper.

Bolan set the little Cayuse down on its mangled skids. It listed as it settled. Bolan motioned for Bobby to get in on the pilot side, while he himself slid over to the copilot controls.

The helicopter was already well back up in the sky under Bolan's control before Bobby had time to close the door.

He was breathless. "Y'know, Colonel," he puffed, "you're...." He was completely at a loss. He gave the Executioner a pound on the shoulder. "How about 'incredible'?"

Bolan acknowledged the vet with a question. "You fly, buddy?"

Latchford briefly regarded the controls. "Hell, yes," he said.

"Great. Do exactly as I tell you."

The blond guy sobered dutifully, his war zone awareness returning. "Yes, sir."

"First, get me across that clearing there. Don't set her down and don't stop. Just get me close enough to jump on the run. Then you and this lady get the hell—"

"What lady?"

"Hi," said a woman's voice. "I'm Anna Charissa."

Bobby looked over his shoulder, then back to Bolan.

"Take damn good care of her, understand?" said the blacksuited nighthawk. "Once you've dropped me, keep right on going. The western perimeter is a soft spot. Go right on through the middle and out. Swing north around the plateau. When you've cleared the plateau, get yourself heading zero-two-four and maintain it, no matter what, until you're intercepted by friendly forces—and I do mean *American* forces. Got it?"

"Maintain heading zero-two-four. Got it, Colonel."

"You're a damn good man, Latchford."

The controls were in Bobby's hands as Bolan snapped fresh clips into each of three weapons.

Bolan pulled out the small radio again and relayed the chopper's flight plan to Grimaldi, on the chance that the fly guy might hear it.

Again, no acknowledgment came from the airborne cavalry.

Latchford was dividing his attention between flying the copter and staring at Bolan's profile, as if trying to place the mystery man's face.

"Now, guy!" shouted Bolan. He opened the door

and balanced himself on the wobbly skid as the Cayuse started down.

Bolan knew it would be a media coup for the ambassador's wife to be personally delivered to safety by one of the kidnapped vets.

The honor would be Latchford's, though it might as well have been Sergeant Larry Shortner, the marine who risked his life to cover the lady's escape, knowing full well he would be beaten or killed for his "tantrum." Shortner surely deserved better treatment than that, and Mack Bolan was on his way to see that he got it.

As the helicopter skimmed across the open space, inches above the ground, the big man in black hit *terra firma* like a cat and set off in a crouching run. He snapped up the Uzi just in time to ruin the earthly life of a terrorist soldier who had just stepped from behind the cover of a barracks building and was taking aim. The aspiring marksman had encountered the Bolan Effect, which had gotten him dispatched to the deep sleep of the big-barracks-in-the-sky.

Bolan charged past the crumpling body, cut around the corner of the building and blasted hot lead into a trio of terrorists firing AK-47s at the fleeing copter. The three men were hurled into each other like falling dominoes, never to know what hit them.

The Cayuse containing the lady and Latchford flew on.

By the time the last body toppled, the Executioner was already one building closer to the big barn.

The double doors on the ground floor banged open and half a dozen terrormakers rumbled out, rifles at the ready.

He was fifteen yards from them. The big night-fighter unclipped a grenade from his belt and flipped it at their feet, then dived in a rolling tumble away from the fire pattern of their frenzied automatic outbursts. He came back to his feet in the same motion, letting fly another grenade just as the first one whumped most of the guards into the next world. The second explosion eliminated the hangers-on.

While other soldiers scrambled to take up positions inside the doorframe, the Executioner was already gone from there and blazing through the second-floor entry on the building's western side.

He catwalked inside, through the deep shadows along the concrete walkway, past the iron-barred cell that had held Anna Charissa only an unbelievable twelve minutes earlier.

The "studio" lights were still blazing, but the two small video cameras stared blankly at the walls.

A stalking apparition reached the top of the concrete steps unseen by the khaki-clad men who held their positions at the double doors across the big open room. They took turns firing out into the darkness, at imagined black apparitions.

Bolan slunk down the stairs and stepped carefully over the mess of cables and wires toward the place where Shortner had been sitting.

The former Green Beret was not exactly sitting now, but he was still in the chair, strapped to it, his body slumped, his head lying to one side. His face was grotesquely distorted in pain. The man was trying to retain consciousness in spite of wicked head wounds and, worse, a pair of mangled legs.

The short-haired sergeant blinked when he saw the man in black. Squinting through watery eyes, he hoarsely managed a whispered, "Knees...."

The poor bastard had been kneecapped.

A few deft slices from the Executioner's blade

released the man from the chair. Shortner did his best to suppress a painful groan, at the same time straining to remain conscious. With tremendous effort the former Green Beret sergeant pulled himself into a sitting position.

The two men consulted each other with eyes only.

Bolan gathered up two broken boards from the busted-up table and fastened them as splints to Shortner's legs with black electrician's tape that was lying on the floor. The men at the far door still blazed into the night.

Then he snatched up Shortner's dropped beret and whispered: "Bite on this."

The sergeant did not have to be told about the pain that was to come. He took Bolan's advice and received the beret between his teeth.

The Executioner slipped the Beretta out of its holster and into Shortner's right hand. After checking to ensure the soldiers were still preoccupied with external apparitions, he grabbed Shortner's left arm and the upper part of his left leg and thrust him over his shoulders in a fireman's lift.

The man's body went limp and Bolan knew he had fainted. But some inner part of Shortner held fast to the gun and the beret, some inner part that perhaps only soldiers knew.

Carrying his human cargo, the bold one avoided the brightness of the stage lights and threaded his way around and through the cameras and other equipment and made it back to the inner stairway. Halfway up, he heard a guard clattering through the upper doorway. He took that as his cue to back off the steps and quietly skirt along the wall beneath the walkway, where he figured to find another door in the dark shadows of a corner.

A single bullet pinged off the wall a few inches in front of his face, showering him and his burden with concrete dust. He turned to see one of the terrorists at the ground-floor double doors urging the other soldiers to swing their weapons around.

Bolan unleashed the belching Uzi on them, then broke into a labored jog just as the surviving terrorists released a flock of flying lead into the place he had just vacated. Bolan legged it around a corner into a blackened corridor that led off from the ground floor. It was a hallway. A hallway with an exit.

Behind him more soldiers took up the chase. Bolan kept moving, pushing for the exit.

He reached it, grabbed the latch and pulled the door open.

He froze. He was staring into the hollow barrel of an automatic pistol. Behind the barrel lurked a pair of hollow eyes.

The eyes were those of Etalo Yareem. The man was back from the hellgrounds and looked it.

A fire, apparently set by the rampaging vets, raged outside the door. Its light poured through the doorway around the crippled terrorist leader. For a moment he stood there in shredded clothing, drenched in his own blood. He had survived the copter crash. His was not the one that had exploded.

A fire of a different sort had erupted in the madman's eyes.

"*You*, mister man in black," he seethed as he cocked back the pistol hammer. "I have found you."

Only a sigh could be heard as the loud report of Yareem's gun, spitting yellow flame into the half-light of the hallway, died down. The useless bullet ricocheted off the cement wall as it passed Bolan and

Shortner and dug into the leg of a dumbfounded terrorist soldier behind them.

The sigh had come from the Beretta, thanks to the
upside-down marksmanship of Sergeant Larry Shortner.

Yareem's pistol had flown out of his fist as he was
spun by the hit. The creep grasped at his wounded
right shoulder and fell back against the edge of the
doorframe.

Meanwhile Bolan lobbed a primed grenade over
his shoulder at the approaching group of terror-
guards howling about the death of their master.
Bolan and Shortner were gone from the scene before
the explosion rocked the concrete construction
around them.

Just outside the big building, the Executioner
turned around to see the slumped form of dying
Etalo Yareem lying in the smoking doorway. Wordlessly, Bolan drew the AutoMag and took careful
aim.

The round was not for mercy. It was just for good.

The outside world had changed considerably in the
few minutes Bolan had been inside the barn. The
whump-whump-whump of at least a dozen large
choppers and as many smaller ones filled the air, a
welcome symphony occasionally punctuated by profound explosions and the sporadic accompaniment
of automatic-weapons fire.

Flames were everywhere in evidence. One of the
barracks buildings had already been leveled, the
other was meeting the same fate at that moment.

The terrorists had broken ranks and were fleeing
into the surrounding jungle, most of them not stopping even to return fire unless the target was directly
between themselves and escape.

Mack Bolan carried his load into the mid-compound clearing, moving toward the helicopters landing there. A grinning Jack Grimaldi ran up out of rotor-swirled smoke and the stroboscopes of battle to help shoulder Shortner's weight.

"Some of the vets are messed up pretty bad," shouted Grimaldi, dropping his grin.

Bolan grunted.

Grimaldi got Sergeant Shortner to a comfortable place in a chopper and strapped him in. The battered man was still drifting in and out of consciousness. His eyes opened now, peering up at Bolan. "Thanks," he said, then handed back the Beretta.

"Yeah, you too, fella," replied the tall man in black, taking the 93-R and holstering it. "You did it all."

"I gotta know," Shortner gasped. "Did you get my signals, you know, on the videotapes?"

"You bet," said a sober Bolan, checking his watch. "Rest up now, Sergeant. You'll be home soon."

Bolan climbed down from the craft, with Grimaldi following. The man they left inside was smiling through all his pain.

Bolan had a question for the flier. "You get my radio signal?"

"No, Sarge. The plateau. There was no way our radios could connect."

"My responsibility, Jack. I should have thought of that."

"You ain't gonna go hard on yourself, are ya, Sarge? I've seen what happens to guys you do that to—they don't generally live too long, right?"

Mack Bolan smiled at his buddy.

A sudden *ack-ack-ack* interrupted him. Flying fast

toward them from the west was another chopper, and a familiar one at that—it was the specially fitted Cayuse that Bolan had borrowed in Panama. Some of the escaping terrorists had stumbled onto it and decided to go out shooting.

"Jeez!" yelled Grimaldi, grabbing for an M-16 inside the chopper. "Sons of bitches!"

Bolan reached into his pocket as Grimaldi took aim. He pulled out a small black box and flicked its little lid open and clicked the switch—all before Jack could take his shot.

Immediately the helicopter became a huge thunderous fireball. It lit the entire compound for seconds before it fell to earth.

Grimaldi's mouth fell open in amazement and disappointment. In the eerie firelight of the hellgrounds, he saw the tiny transmitter box and the big man's grin. The hot-tempered flier shot a buddy-punch to the Executioner's big shoulder.

"You bastard," he laughed.

EPILOGUE

HAL BROGNOLA PUNCHED BUTTONS on the console in front of him. In response, the video image winked out on the big screen across the room. Hal moved to the window and pulled open the sashes, admitting the bright Memorial Day sun into the War Room.

They had gathered there, all of them, the warrior and his support-system members, to view a live transmission from the White House, a broadcast also witnessed by almost every home in the country.

The president of the United States had expressed his sorrow over the death of the American ambassador to the United Nations, John Leonard Charissa, whom he called a trusted friend.

Next, he introduced a serene Anna Charissa, now safely delivered from terrorism. He asked her to accept the role of her late husband as United States Ambassador to the U.N.

Finally, the president introduced his newest advisers, two men whom he charged with the responsibility of developing workable solutions, at whatever cost, to the personal readjustment problems of every soldier who had served in the conflict known as Vietnam—regardless of their discharge codes, honorable or not. The men he named to this specially created Presidential Commission were Larry Shortner, who then appeared and waved from a wheelchair, and Bobby Latchford, who stepped forward and stood proudly.

PRIOR TO THE BROADCAST, the Stony Man assembly had watched some bizarre video outtakes, courtesy of the Central Intelligence Agency. The impounded scenes included one of Anna Charissa being roughly *removed* from the C-130. There was also a hilarious sequence showing the two "pilots" repeatedly pretending to jump out of the back of the transport plane, including a take in which one of them snagged the black "night" curtain hanging outside the cargo door and pulled it down as he fell.

The pilots did, of course, bail out of the plane after it took off, but by then there were no cameras. And, of course, no Anna Charissa. The transport's actual passenger was a mannequin.

When the president's broadcast ended, April Rose stood up.

"Well," she began brightly. "With everyone here at the same time, this really does seem like a holiday."

"A damned hard holiday," offered Leo Turrin, to general agreement from Carl Lyons, Jack Grimaldi, Aaron Kurtzman, Gadgets Schwarz and Pol Blancanales.

All heads turned to the blue eyes in the corner.

Mack Bolan faced them, hands in pockets, legs at ease.

"My friends," he said, his powerful voice relaxed and laconic. "What does not kill us only makes us stronger. Today has been tough. Today we're strong as hell."

MACK BOLAN

THE EXECUTIONER 52

BOLAN

appears again in
Tuscany Terror

Crazed Communist terrorists have kidnapped the wife
and infant daughter of a U.S. Army officer in Italy.
Unless the American officer "confesses" to NATO
involvement with the Italian Mafia, his family will
become the latest gruesome statistics in the annals of
modern terrorism.

For the big guy, this will be his gutsiest scrap yet, a
merciless search-and-destroy mission. He will
unleash his own kind of blistering death.

Let the bastards beware. . . .

Coming soon:

MACK BOLAN FIGHTS ALONGSIDE ABLE TEAM AND PHOENIX FORCE

in

STONY MAN DOCTRINE

20 million hostages!

In ten days of bloodletting, a diabolical revolutionary junta determines to soften up the United States.

Their purpose? Pave the way for a massive invasion.

Led by a terrifying troika—three brutal maniacs for whom no act of violence is an outrage— the barbarian army attacks five carefully selected American "communities."

The result? Horror and carnage.

For the first time, Mack Bolan joins with his counterterror groups—Able Team and Phoenix Force—to wage war against the ultimate holocaust. Nine brave men have ten days to stem a truly terrible tide.

THIS IS THE BIG ONE!

Available soon wherever paperbacks are sold.

GOLD EAGLE

MACK BOLAN

THE EXECUTIONER SERIES

I am not their judge. I am their judgment—I am their executioner.
— *Mack Bolan,*
a.k.a. Col. John Phoenix

Mack Bolan is the free world's leading force in the new Terrorist Wars, defying all terrorists and destroying them piece by piece, using his Vietnam-trained tactics and knowledge of jungle warfare. Bolan's new war is the most exciting series ever to explode into print. You won't want to miss a single word. Start your collection now!

"This is a publishing marvel. Stores have a hard time keeping these books in stock!"
— *The Orlando Voice*

#39 The New War
#40 Double Crossfire
#41 The Violent Streets
#42 The Iranian Hit
#43 Return to Vietnam
#44 Terrorist Summit

#45 Paramilitary Plot
#46 Bloodsport
#47 Renegade Agent
#48 The Libya Connection
#49 Doomsday Disciples
#50 Brothers in Blood

GOLD
EAGLE

Available wherever paperbacks are sold.

Mack Bolan's

ABLE TEAM

AN EXECUTIONER SERIES

by Dick Stivers

In the fire-raking tradition of The Executioner, Able Team's Carl Lyons, Pol Blancanales and Gadgets Schwarz are the three hotshots who avenge terror with screaming silvered fury. They are the Death Squad reborn, and their long-awaited adventures are the best thing to happen since the Mack Bolan and the Phoenix Force series. Collect them all! They are classics of their kind! Do not miss these titles!

"Written in the inimitable Executioner style!"
—*Mystery News*

#1 Tower of Terror
#2 The Hostaged Island
#3 Texas Showdown

#4 Amazon Slaughter
#5 Cairo Countdown

Able Team titles are available wherever paperbacks are sold.

GOLD EAGLE

Mack Bolan's

PHOENIX FORCE

AN EXECUTIONER SERIES

by Gar Wilson

Phoenix Force is The Executioner's five-man army
that blazes through the dirtiest of encounters. Like
commandos who fight for the love of battle and the
righteous unfolding of the logic of war, Bolan's five
hardasses make mincemeat out of their enemies.
Catch up on the whole series now!

"Strong-willed and true. Gold Eagle Books are
making history. Full of adventure, daring and
action!"

—*Marketing Bestsellers*

GOLD EAGLE

Phoenix Force titles are available
wherever paperbacks are sold.

Mack Samuel Bolan, strong American—proud enough to prove to the world that one good man is worth a billion terrorists

"About a month ago I was introduced to the life of Mack Bolan. I have pulled the trigger when he has, released the mortar shell when he has—I am enveloped in the character of the Executioner."

—T.B., New York, NY

"Mack has become part of my life, like a brother. A couple of guys at work follow him as closely as I do, and we will be Bolan fans no matter what his new name, or what new enemy he fights!"

—C.D., Elyria, OH

"I have read various books throughout my life but there is something about the Executioner that makes me a loyal fan—in the Bolan books I see *truth*. Thank you!"

—G.B., USSDD Eisenhower

"For me, John Phoenix displays an almost perfect awareness—a sense of balance, moral correctness, and a great depth of character."

—L.D., Canoga Park, California

"The most exciting hero of our times."

—H.R., Watertown, New York